ALL HER DREAMS
OF LOVE

Infused with a wealth of knowledge of 19th-century Southern life, Mary Lou Cheatham weaves an emotionally satisfying tale in a style reminiscent of Harper Lee.

>Regina Rodgers,
>
>Author of *The Gamble on Love*

Mary Lou Cheatham writes wonderful stories with rich characters, interesting settings, and true-to-life plot lines. Be sure to read *All Her Dreams of Love* and get caught up in Nancy O'Reilly's world.

>Jackie Zack,
>
>Author of *An Irish Heart*

Another heartwarming historical romance by Mary Lou Cheatham. Jeb and Nancy meet amid tragic happenings in their lives. Both fight the growing attraction between them due to society's expectations during their day. A well-told story.

>Jonni Rich
>
>Author of *The Chartres House Murders*

For My Niece

Susan Shepard

All Her Dreams of Love

Mary Lou Cheatham

Copyright © 2023
Mary G. Cooke
All Rights Reserved

No part of this book may be reproduced or transmitted in any form or by any means, electronic or mechanical, including photocopying, recording, or by any information storage and retrieval system without the written permission of the author, except where permitted by law.

ISBN : 979-8858411437

Table of Contents

Chapter 1 1
Chapter 2 13
Chapter 3 26
Chapter 4 35
Chapter 5 44
Chapter 6 52
Chapter 7 59
Chapter 8 70
Chapter 9 83
Chapter 10 90
Chapter 11 97
Chapter 12 108
Chapter 13 119
Chapter 14 130
Chapter 15 139
Chapter 16 144
Chapter 17 146
Chapter 18 159
Chapter 19 167
Chapter 20 172
Chapter 21 180
Chapter 22 195
Chapter 23 203
Chapter 24 212

Chapter 25	223
Chapter 26	235
Chapter 27	239
Chapter 28	245
Chapter 29	262
Chapter 30	271
Chapter 31	279
Chapter 32	289
Chapter 33	295
About the Author	297
Acknowledgements	298

Chapter 1

"Is Papa coming home today?"

Nancy smiled at her son's eager face. She couldn't say for sure. "He always comes home on Friday. I don't know exactly when he'll get here, Tommy. Let's make sure we have everything ready for him."

Tommy blinked back tears. "I miss him so much."

Nancy hugged him. "I do too, sweetheart."

"The time needs to pass fast for me so I won't have to be sad."

"Me too." She straightened Tommy's collar. "If it passes too fast though, we won't be ready."

It's been a busy week for us. So many things to tell Amos.

"Mama?"

She swept the porch one more time. "Yes, dear."

"Do you think Papa will notice we whitewashed the house?"

"Yes, I do, and I think he'll notice we put cucumbers in the crock to make pickles."

Tommy snickered. "He'll notice them pickles all right. They stink."

"I doubt he'll notice we've harvested a little corn."

She'd coax him to tell her about his week, then kiss him softly.

The big burly man would throw down the bag on his back containing dirty clothes to be laundered. And he'd lift Tommy high. As Amos whirled the boy around, he would say, "Son, I declare you've grown an inch taller this week."

While the sun lowered, Nancy and Tommy waited on the front porch. The aroma of the pecan pie cooling in the kitchen wafted through the open window. The day had been good. After a short nap, Tommy dug some earthworms from the worm bed and dropped them into a little bucket stuffed with dirt. They grabbed their cane poles. That afternoon at Cohay Creek they caught a mess of yellow-throated bream. Tommy helped remove the scales from the three fish he caught.

Nancy removed the heads and gutted the fish while he watched. "What a fine little man you are. Soon you'll be catching more fish than I can."

Now that the fish were ready to be fried, the cows turned into the night pasture from their milking stalls, and the mules and pigs fed, she sat rocking in a chair to cool off.

Tommy built a miniature house with his blocks of multiple shapes and sizes. Construction of the blocks represented an ongoing project in which Amos taught Tommy to draw lines and cut along them. After they sawed them, Tommy sanded them smooth. It had been fun watching Amos teach his boy carpentry skills.

The blue calico dress she needed to hem slipped from her fingers. "Me and your pa have got big plans. We're working hard to get ahead. One day we're going to build a fine house. Another thing - we're saving up money so you can get a good education."

As she stared down the lane cutting through the trees, she listened for her husband's excellent singing voice to fill the air with a melodic rendition of "Home, Sweet Home." When he approached, he'd be wearing a big smile showing he was happy.

"There's no place like home." She crooned until her soft alto voice broke. The old clock her father had given her chimed inside the house. Time played a dirty trick.

Her little boy came and laid his hands on her lap. "Where's Papa?"

"He'll show up directly." Placing her work-worn, calloused hands over his, she hoped the six-year-old didn't hear the shaking in her voice.

Tommy turned one ear toward the road. "I hear Pa."

"I thought I did too." She listened. "No, it was our imagination."

"'Cause we want to hear him so bad?" Tommy frowned.

"That's right."

"I heard a gunshot."

She laughed. "It was probably B. K. shooting hawks trying to steal his chickens."

"No, ma'am." Tommy pointed to the left. "The Barneses live that way, but the shot came from the other direction."

Tommy's words sent a chill through her body. It wasn't unusual to hear gunshots. Farmers shot predatory animals. Not much hunting took place in the hot weather. She tried to conceal the tension she felt.

The flame-colored sunset fading into ash gray signaled to the O'Reillys' chickens it was time for them to roost inside their house. The big white dog, old Grover, came in from a chase for his supper and sank in a ball near Nancy's chair.

She couldn't put her finger on it, but something was off. The air felt strange.

Darkness seeped in from under the trees. Still no Amos. She arose. After stretching her exhausted frame, she studied every inch of the road. "Stack your blocks against the wall so folks won't trip."

He knocked down the house he'd built. Nancy ignored the slight tantrum as she waited for the child to place the blocks in a neat row next to the wall. Tommy shook his head like an old man. "Wouldn't want Papa to trip on them in the dark."

Inside the kitchen, a big front room that also served as a dining room and sitting room, Nancy turned the round disc to bring kerosene into the wick of the lamp. She lit it, placed the glass globe over the flame, and adjusted the light.

She stirred the fire and added wood from the box. "Let's fry up the fish."

"If Papa would have gotten here on time, me and him could have fried the fish in the yard. The stove is going to make it hot in here."

She dredged the fish in meal seasoned with salt and black pepper. "He'll be here directly."

Butterbeans with dumplings stayed warm in an iron pot. Nancy whipped up some cornmeal fritters, which she dropped by spoonfuls into the bubbling lard. Two small glasses of buttermilk graced the table. It was important to drink some milk every day because of the baby on the way. A plate with cutlery and a homemade cloth napkin remained set for Amos.

Nancy took pride in her ability to coordinate a meal. All the food was ready at the same moment. They served their plates and paused to say grace.

She prayed, "Dear Father in heaven, we are thankful to have this food before us. We thank you for the hard work Amos does as he provides for us through his labor. Please protect and guide him as he makes his way back from the lumber mill. Bless this meal and our home. Watch over the Barneses. Thank you for our wonderful neighbors."

Tommy prayed, "Thank you, God, for this food and for my mama and papa. Please keep my papa safe and bring him home soon. Thank you for always being with us. In Jesus' name. Amen."

Nancy drank her buttermilk and ate some beans with only a few bites of fish. They sat in silence and kept looking out the window for an approaching light.

Afterwards, Tommy scraped the plates and placed them on the table beside the dishpan. She washed the dishes in soapy water and stacked them in another pan.

Everything had to be done in the correct order if Nancy had any hope for her family to stay healthy. First, she washed the glasses, then the plates, next the cutlery. A kettle of hot water poured over the dishes sanitized them. Finally, the cookware rendered the dishwater a murky mess. She emptied the pan of gray water into a bucket on the back porch. In the morning, she'd throw it into the hogs' watering trough.

Her son dried the dishes, then wiped the brown oilcloth table covering and hung the towel on a peg.

After they cleaned the dishes, Tommy went to his room and returned. He'd washed his face and changed into his nightshirt. He sat by Nancy on the settee, and she read a chapter of *The Adventures of Tom Sawyer*. He watched every word. Next she read the Bible. When her eyes blurred and her voice quaked, Tommy finished the twenty-third Psalm.

She hugged him and kissed his cheek. "Off to bed."

"Come tuck me in."

She pulled the sheet up around him. Tommy prayed, "I'm so worried, God, but I trust you to take care of Papa and us."

As Nancy started to leave Tommy's room, he asked, "Where's Papa?"

She spoke in a determined tone as she twirled a lock of her hair. "He'll be here directly."

Amos will come home to me and Tommy. I need him to help me with the baby I'm carrying... I love this man.

As soon as Tommy settled into the heavy breaths of sleep, Nancy slipped onto the porch and sat in a rocking chair under the light of the buttery full moon. She didn't feel so good. The few bites of fish gave her indigestion. *Listen for Amos...forget the misery I feel...*

He should have been coming down the road. Instead, the sounds of the night - whippoorwills, bobcats, and the screaming panther - added to her sense of isolation and loneliness. The panther reminded her that Amos could have encountered danger.

As the night creatures mocked her, Grover ambled over to her chair.

"Hi, Grover." She scratched his white fur. "You're my loyal companion. Guarding the front porch. Helping out on the farm as you know how. Thank you, Lord, for this sweet old dog."

She waited in silence.

The debris under the nearby trees rattled as the leaves made crunching noises.

Grover stood and raised his hackles.

"Amos?"

No answer.

"Steady, boy." She placed her hand on the dog's collar. "Stay."

Furry brown creatures with black and white facial markings stepped from the shadows. A family of mischievous-looking raccoons, consisting of a mother leading two young ones, sniffed around.

Grover threatened them with a growl.

"Oh, so you're exploring. Looking for some table scraps."

When the night settled again, Nancy went inside. She lit a candle and turned out the kerosene lamp. On the way to bed, she tiptoed into Tommy's room. His angelic face looked peaceful in the light of the moon beaming in through the window.

Inside her room, she changed into her lightweight yellow cotton nightgown with short sleeves and a low neckline, which allowed for airflow. A homespun bedspread, woven by her grandmother, covered her bed. Nancy called her Granny. As usual, Nancy folded it and laid it on a chair.

The candle, snuffed out, stood on her bedside table. The feather bed caressed her tired body as she pulled a muslin sheet up for cover.

When had she ever been so lonely? The night before and the ones before that, it had been just Tommy and her, but the situation had felt different. They had Amos to look forward to on the weekend.

The moon passed its light through the white curtains trimmed in lace. Amos had given her the lace as a Christmas present the first year after they married. They had a lovely home. Her hand reached between the nightstand and her bed to touch the double-barreled shotgun she kept handy to protect her from predators. Her only fear was that something bad had happened to Amos.

Nancy prayed silently. *Dear God, please bring my beloved home safely. Give me the strength to endure this uncertainty, the peace to pass on to Tommy, and the faith that everything will work out for the best.*

Bless the child we are expecting. Please watch over my husband and guide him home to me. Let him know I love him. Tears streamed sideways as she lay on her back.

Without Amos, I won't be able to carry on.

She dreamed she and Amos stood on a bluff overlooking Cohay Creek. He held her tenderly.

As tired as she was, the night passed quickly.

In the light of the morning, her hand reached to the pillow on the other side of the bed.

Empty. The hope that Amos could have slipped into the house during the night was also empty.

Tommy in his nightshirt came to her bedside. "Good morning, Mama."

"Good morning." She stood beside her bed. "Go outside and close the door behind you. I'll be out in a minute."

She opened the little cedar jewelry box on her bureau. It was a ritual to make sure her wedding ring with its little emerald stone and the brooch that Granny had given her were in the box. She wore her jewelry to church and to the mercantile, but she didn't want to risk losing or soiling them when she did farm chores. The brooch and the picture propped nearby were all she had of Ma. Someone had painted it when her mother was young. Ma had wavy blonde hair like Nancy's.

She pulled on her robe and went to the kitchen. Breakfast consisted of milk from a jug she'd placed in a bucket of water overnight, eggs boiled the day before, leftover biscuits with butter, and blackberry jam. It was a quick meal requiring little preparation. "We need to get on with the chores soon."

Tommy set down his half-empty glass of milk. "Why aren't you eating?"

"I will." Nancy nibbled at her biscuit.

"When's Papa coming home?"

"Directly." She bolted through the door. Standing on the edge of the porch as she steadied herself by holding onto a porch post, she emptied the contents of her stomach.

What must Tommy have thought of her going outside to relieve her upset belly?

They dressed for the day and went to the barnyard. Tommy climbed into the crib and shucked a few of last year's nubbins, which he threw out to the chickens for them to peck.

Nancy milked Flossie and Bella and turned them out to pasture. She took the lard cans of milk to the cool cellar.

They freshened up. Their hands washed and hair combed, they readied themselves for the day ahead.

"What we gonna do, Mama?"

"Go look for your pa." She rubbed some butter on her work-worn face and secured her hair in a bun. "We won't go far." As soon as the butter soaked into her skin, she put on her bonnet. Her long-sleeved dress would protect her from the sun.

Tommy wore long sleeves and short pants. His sunhat rested securely on his head with a cord to keep it from blowing away.

From her bedside, she took her shotgun while Tommy grabbed his slingshot and a few rocks.

As they stepped onto the front porch, a strange contraption, possibly living quarters, atop a wagon frame stood parked in the driveway. A large man stepped out of the front and pulled a tiny girl from the seat into his arms.

Chapter 2

"Hush, Grover." Nancy reached for the dog and missed. "What's the matter with you?" She grabbed his collar and tried to restrain him, but he wiggled free and ran to the back of the wagon. Another dog inside it engaged in a barking contest with him.

When the tall, broad-shouldered stranger dropped the reins, the horses stood still as though grateful for the rest. He didn't tie them to the hitching post.

"Howdy, ma'am." He removed his hat and held it respectfully. Curly auburn hair blew all directions in the morning breeze. "My name is Jeb, and this here's my little one, Evie."

Nancy grasped her shotgun with the stock on the ground as she stared at the ragged fellow and his bizarre wagon, made of wood painted green. Pegs on the front of the dilapidated structure held pots and pans, hoes and saws, a hunter's horn tied by a cord, a rifle, and a guitar. The traveler's blue chambray work shirt and bib overalls looked as though they could stand to be boiled in a washpot. The pungent whiff of Jeb and his clothing drifted all the way to the porch. He must have ridden a long way.

"You're at the O'Reilly house. I'm Nancy O'Reilly, and this is my son Tommy." If Amos had come home, she would have reached out to the shy child. Under the circumstances, she didn't have time to waste. In a dismissive tone, she asked, "What can we do for you?"

"I be looking for a piece of property I purchased. According to the courthouse clerk, it borders on the Amos O'Reilly place." He held his hat with one hand while he made expressive gestures with the other. "The land's left a-lying fallow for many a year."

The way he drew out his words and spoke with a lilt revealed he'd come from North Carolina. He must have traveled for weeks. Might he have run into Amos on the road? "Yes, the place borders our fence. The gate took you into our property."

He stood the little girl beside him, and she wrapped her arms around his leg. "Much obliged."

"Amos, he's my husband. He ought to be here directly." She couldn't afford to let him know the man of the house was missing.

His penetrating gaze, resting first on her eyes and traveling to her mouth, made her fidget. Did he know she held a secret about the absence of Amos?

The child shook her head causing her crown of strawberry-colored ringlets to bounce like cork screws. She looked from one face to another with her enormous eyes and puckered her small pouty mouth. Her streaked face indicated someone had tried to wash it with a dirty rag. Her flowered dress, with ripped lace, needed laundering.

The little travel-weary family needed help, and Nancy believed it was her duty to show hospitality to strangers who came to her home. At the moment, though, she needed to take care of her own family first. If Amos had come home, she would have served a meal, and maybe after they became a little better acquainted, offered to bathe the child.

Her hands itched to launder and mend Evie's dress, but her heart told her she must look for Amos. "Pleased to meet you. I suppose you're talking about the Forbess place."

"That's right. Hulen Forbess." He shifted his weight from one leg to the other and tousled Evie's hair.

"Mr. Hulen died in the war, and his family moved on. I don't know where you're from or why you're parked in front of our house, but you'd best be on your way." After she leaned her gun against the side of the porch, Nancy pulled on her bonnet and tied it in place. "We've got work to do."

"Yes, ma'am." He lifted the girl into the wagon. "Pleasure meeting y'all too. I want to have a word with Amos. Maybe next time."

Nancy shushed Tommy with an upheld hand. She lifted her shotgun and propped it on her shoulder, barrels pointing behind her.

The man stretched his long, muscled legs as he boarded the wagon again and drove his team away.

"Remember, Tommy, we don't tell folks your pa ain't here."

He laughed. "I know, Mama. We lie. I mean we tell stories."

"Not exactly." How could she teach him to be honest and at the same time have him participate in her little ruse?

Tommy's grin was full of mischief. "When somebody suspicious comes up to our place, I'm supposed to call out to Papa like he's inside the house even though he ain't home."

Nancy pushed loose tendrils of hair behind her ears. She wished Tommy wouldn't say things that put her on the spot. "Right."

"That's what I was fixing to do. But then I thought better of it. You'd done give away our secret."

Nancy darted back inside and grabbed her reticule. She and Tommy, with Grover following, went to catch the mules.

Tommy brought out a few nubbins of corn to entice them, and Nancy carried their bridles. Without much effort they captured the team of mules and hitched them to the wagon.

They rode to the edge of their property. She hoped to see some sign of Amos. He may have grown so tired that he sat down to rest when he was almost home. If he was exhausted after working at the sawmill all day, then walking miles, he could have decided to sit for a minute. He may have fallen asleep. It was unlikely, though, that he stopped. He would have pushed on until he reached the house.

"Let's go up to the church," Tommy suggested.

"Okay." A ride through the church grounds would probably not provide any clues about Amos's disappearance. It could, however, bring peaceful thoughts and happy memories to both Nancy and Tommy.

They rode on toward the church. The road wound through tall loblolly pines growing so close they blocked the sunlight. Nancy slowed to look under every tree. She'd heard stories of people who had epileptic seizures and passed out in the woods. Or maybe he experienced sudden death from a snakebite. All kinds of dreadful possibilities arose within her mind. Leaving the trees behind, the road carried them to fields on either side. Lush grass soon to turn brown and cut for hay rippled in the breeze.

No sign of Amos. The reality of what was happening sent her into panic. How could the countryside look so beautiful when she suffered such anxiety? She brought her hand to her chest as her heart hammered in despair and she gasped for breath.

For Tommy's sake, she had to hold her head high. As her sense of helplessness grew stronger, she fought back the tears and bit her lip. There was nothing she could do to help Amos.

The road curved sharply to the left and led them up a hill. To the right was the cemetery, and to the left was the church, which had ample grounds for wagons and surreys to park on Sundays. Every other Sunday, the preacher came to lead the worship services. On the alternate Sundays, the deacons and musicians led a service of hymn singing and Bible reading. This was the week when the preacher would attend.

She turned off the red clay road and drove the mules around the building. "You fellows must be confused. We just need to look around."

Tommy chuckled. "The mules are pretty smart."

When she had completed her circle around the church, she stopped at the front. "Son, hop down and go over to see if the door is locked. Don't go inside. All I want you to do is to see if the door will open."

"Okay, Mama."

She felt a sensation of dread in the pit of her stomach. What if Tommy went to the door and it was unlocked? What if she'd sent him into danger?

It was locked.

Nancy turned left instead of right as they left the churchyard.

Tommy looked up at her. "Where you headed?"

"To the settlement. Since we're almost there, I thought we'd go on to the mercantile." Now that Amos had broken the routine, she'd need to break it too. Instead of doing Saturday morning work in the garden or the fields then eating dinner at noon and going to the store, she'd go early.

She drove the mules down the hill toward Lyon Creek. There was a steep drop-off on the left, and the road took a sharp left turn. Fields of corn, now turning brown, covered the flat land. In the blistering wind, the cornstalks rattled.

Every time she'd gone to the mercantile, men were shooting dice under a shade tree. Amos had told her they were no-goods, men too lazy to farm. He said they hoped to make a living winning at the games, but their behavior made no sense.

That Saturday morning, no men shot dice in the shade of the tree. The idlers were nowhere to be seen. Did the game start after noon? Or had they gone elsewhere?

Nancy parked near the entrance to the store and hitched the mule team to the post. "Grover, stay. Guard the wagon."

Grover stepped to the side of the wagon and assumed his duty. Inside, she selected hoop cheese, flour, lard, baking soda, salt, and a dozen crackers from the barrel. She let Tommy choose a stick of peppermint candy.

"That's all you need today?" Felton Oglethorpe, the owner, asked.

Despite her disappointment that Amos was missing, Nancy felt a flash of amusement at Felton's appearance. Unlike the other men, who dressed in bib overalls and brogans, the store owner wore a white shirt with garters on his arms to keep his shirt sleeves from falling down too long. As usual, he had a red polka dot bow tie, which was askew. Pleated trousers with wide legs and a skinny belt finished his attire. He wore shiny black shoes.

"Yes." Nancy pulled money from her reticule. Because Amos brought his pay home every week, she had the means to pay cash, unlike some of the neighbors who bought on credit. But what if Amos never returned? She'd need to shop sparingly. She could bring vegetables from the garden and eggs to help pay her bill.

He loaded the supplies into the wagon. "Give Amos my regards."

She thanked him and with Tommy at her side drove the wagon back home.

Since Amos usually came with her, Mr. Oglethorpe didn't have a reason to load the supplies. Was he being overly solicitous or simply nice? His pale skin indicated he seldom stepped out of the mercantile and into the sunshine. His complexion reminded her of paste. Why was he loading her purchases into her wagon?

Where could Amos be? He was not the kind of man who would take his money and leave his family behind. Had he fallen into a hole? Did wild animals attack him? How odd that the men who shot dice games every Saturday were absent.

Back home, she stopped near the porch. They unloaded the purchases, turned the mules into the pasture, and put up the wagon. For lunch they ate crackers and cheese.

They put away the purchased items and took naps. Afterwards, they gathered vegetables from the garden. She picked up some shriveled bean pods. "The pole beans look a little dry. Let's carry some buckets of water from the cistern."

They managed small buckets. Granny had cautioned her not to lift heavy weights when she was carrying Tommy, but this time she had no choice. Except for nausea, indigestion, and fatigue, she had no problems.

Tommy poured the water next to the plants as she had instructed him last week.

"That's right, son. Pour the water gently. Don't get too close."

When they finished the garden chores, she asked Tommy if he'd like to go for a walk.

"Yes, ma'am. We can go look for Papa."

With Grover circling them, they walked side by side to the gate, each with a stick in case they saw snakes.

The lane they'd traveled that morning led to the church and the mercantile. To the left, a narrow road just big enough for a wagon trailed toward the old Forbess place. They took that route because Papa walked this way sometimes when he wanted to take a shortcut.

It had been years since she'd walked over to the Forbess place although it was close by. "Tommy, you've never been up here, have you?"

"Papa took me one time. He went to look around."

A clue to Amos's disappearance could be anywhere. Her eyes examined every bush and track in the sand. "Wagon tracks. Probably the new people."

The house site was clear of trees, but a few scattered bushes had sprung up. Daylilies bloomed in a brilliant array over what had been the front yard. Lush grass covered the surrounding fallow fields.

Tommy pointed at the low stout logs that had served as the foundation for the house to sit on. "Papa said the boards of the house disappeared a few at a time."

"Right, and the thieves stole the boards until the house vanished."

"We got some mean neighbors, Mama."

A rotting well stand barely covered the well beside what must have been the edge of the house. Nancy cautioned Tommy, "Don't go near that well. It's dangerous."

The structures in the back - top of a root cellar, smokehouse, small corn crib, two stables, wagon shed, tool shed, outhouse, and a barn farther behind - stood in various states of collapse.

At the grind of approaching wagon wheels Grover whined and barked. Nancy scolded him until he came and stood behind her although he continued to bark and whimper at intervals.

Jeb and Evie arrived in their wagon. A black dog smaller than Grover ran alongside the wagon. When they came closer, the dog woofed.

Jeb took a harsh tone. "Hush, Cleopatra. Get over here."

The need to keep the secret of Amos's absence outweighed the question as to whether Jeb had seen Amos on the road. She folded the brim of her bonnet back and attempted to speak in a natural tone as she tried to keep her voice smooth without a quiver so Jeb wouldn't suspect anything. "We was out for a stroll. I see y'all found your property."

He pulled back on his reins, tipped his hat to Nancy, and reached for his child. "Come here, Evie. When we get down, don't step too near the horses. Quiet, Cleo."

Nancy and Tommy gazed at the man and his daughter as they climbed out of the wagon. They stood and stared until Jeb looked at them with questioning eyes. "What can I do for you?"

"Oh, nothing." She started to walk away. "We was just leaving. Have a pleasant afternoon."

"Right neighborly for you to drop by." Jeb laughed.

Why did he find the situation amusing? He must have known something she didn't.

On the way home, Nancy took Tommy's hand and squeezed it. "I'm not ready to tell anybody your papa is missing."

Tears rolled down Tommy's cheeks. "Mama, I'm so scared."

After chores and supper, they moved out to the porch. Tommy picked up a handful of blocks and threw them down. Nancy and Tommy watched for Amos until the sun slipped below the trees.

In the darkness of her bed, she cried herself to sleep. Dreams of Amos frightened her.

As the clock struck midnight, she awakened. The words, "Joy cometh in the morning," came to her mind, but she didn't expect any joy. Sunday she'd take a different approach to search for Amos.

Chapter 3

A forlorn chime. One o'clock. Nancy dozed again until Grover's lonesome howl awakened her. Near the house an owl released a *who*. The chickens clucked in an upset conversation. Amos had made the henhouse impervious to all creatures except snakes. Most nights when Nancy went to bed, she thanked God for his tender mercies and the security of the protection provided her by Amos's management skills.

Unaware of his whereabouts, she lost her sense of safety. Her feather bed developed lumps from her constant rolling and tossing.

The clock struck two. Somewhere out there her beloved suffered from an unknown peril.

Lord, this is more than I can handle.

Nancy left her bed at five and made a pan of biscuits. If Amos came home, she'd have something hot and fresh to feed him. After breakfast, she rushed through the milking and feeding. She dressed fast for church and helped her son. Then they took off.

With Tommy by her side, Nancy pulled her mule wagon onto the church premises before anyone else arrived. She parked under the shade tree closest to the door. The grounds filled fast because it was preaching Sunday. After she tied the team to a limb of the tree, she stood waiting for Reverend Barlow while Tommy talked to a group of boys nearby.

"Is Amos ailing?" Josephine, nosy woman she was, asked the question that was none of her business.

Nancy didn't have an answer. She busied herself adjusting her hat. "Morning, Josephine."

"*Well?*" Josephine's voice reached a high pitch as she slapped her hands against her skirt and approached Nancy.

William pulled his wife back. "Come on, woman. Let's go inside."

A stream of others passed. The men tipped their hats to Nancy, and women nodded with sympathetic looks as the children gawked.

Oglethorpe, his black hair parted in the middle and greased in place and his thin moustache freshly waxed, stopped in front of her. "I trust you were able to get your heavy loads unpacked yesterday."

"Yes."

He peered into her face with his green-gray eyes that looked enormous inside his wire-rimmed spectacles. The merchant showed a little too much interest in her situation. What did he know?

At last, Reverend Barlow and Susanna with their three little girls rounded the building.

As Nancy's hands shook and her voice trembled, she walked toward him. "Brother Barlow, I must have a word with you."

"All right, Sister." He glanced at the door. "After the service."

Nancy stepped in front of him. "It can't wait."

The pastor looked heavenward. "What is it?"

"My husband Amos didn't come home Friday night."

"So sorry." He clasped his Bible. "These things happen. I've never known him to partake of spirits, but I suppose he could have yielded to temptation."

"No. You don't understand." She shook her head. "He's missing. Something's terrible wrong."

"Oh, Lord, we beseech thee." He removed his white handkerchief from his pocket and wiped his glasses. "Nancy, we'll do all we can."

Tommy, who stood in front of his mother, squinted with tears and bright sunlight in his eyes. He turned his face up to Reverend Barlow.

She started over. "He didn't come home Friday night from work at the lumber mill south of Mize."

Reverend Barlow tugged at his whiskers. "Seems I've heard him say he works all week and walks home on Friday."

Nancy cried hard. "Yes, but it ain't like him not to show up. I don't know where he is or what's happened to him."

He placed an arm around her trembling shoulders. "Now go on in and take a seat."

As she walked inside and found places for her and her son, she didn't make eye contact with anyone.

Miss Susanna walked to the piano bench, sat, and arranged her skirt with a flourish. She played the introduction to an unfamiliar song. The pastor stood by the piano, and his voice boomed a melodic rendition of "The Ninety and Nine."

>There were ninety and nine that safely lay
>
>In the shelter of the fold;
>
>But one was out on the hills away,
>
>Far off from the gates of gold.
>
>Away on the mountains wild and bare;
>
>Away from the tender Shepherd's care.

After he finished the song, he paused, then walked to the pulpit. "Brothers and sisters, one of our flock is missing. We believe he's out there somewhere in distress. In just a moment we're going to disband this service. All of you that are able-bodied will walk out and form a chain. Those of you who cannot may wait here while we search for our beloved Amos O'Reilly. As you know, he's a faithful Christian man, a good husband and father, and a generous provider. He works at the

Mize lumber mill and walks home every Friday night. Last Friday, he didn't come home though. We don't know whether he met with foul play. Anyway, we'll do what we can this morning to find him. Hand-in-hand, we'll go out and look for the next two hours. God bless you. I'll dismiss us with a prayer."

Most of the men, some of the women, and the older children formed a chain of people that swept down the road and through the woods. Nancy gained strength from her participation in the chain. Tommy was perhaps the youngest child in the group. When trees blocked their way, they dropped hands and joined back up afterwards.

After the two hours that would have been spent in worship, the group returned to the church.

Deacon Harold Harter approached Nancy. "Us deacons will come back and search some more. We plan to assemble at three o'clock in your yard if that's okay with you."

She smiled through her tears.

Nancy needed to inform the law about her husband's disappearance, but the sheriff maintained his headquarters in the county seat sixteen miles away. The only practical means she had to communicate with him was through the mail.

After she and Tommy ate leftover biscuits with cane syrup, she sat at her writing desk to pen a letter and apply a stamp. Tomorrow, she'd mail it at the mercantile.

At three o'clock, when the five deacons drove their wagons into her front yard, their wives came with them. The women brought children, food, and endless chatter. Nancy didn't want any of it, but Granny had taught her how to be gracious. Tommy would benefit from having playmates for a change.

Nancy stepped onto the porch and greeted her guests.

"Whoa!" Harold Harter pulled back on the reins of his wagon in front of her house. "We plan to go on the road and space ourselves. Each man will get out and walk around on the south side of the road."

"It sounds like a good plan." Standing hunched over and arms folded, she shivered at a vision of her husband tied and left somewhere by outlaws. "Amos takes a path through the woods south of the road."

Harter removed his sunhat and wiped his brow. "So, here's what we'll do. We'll hitch our wagons quarter of a mile apart and look along the path."

"I like that idea."

He called to the wagon behind him. "Send the word on back. We're gonna check out the path south of the road."

The men drove off in their wagons. The women chatted, and the children romped. Nancy sat on the swing. She tried to take part - tried not to stare into the woods or to fidget.

After two hours passed, the men returned. "Nothing. Not a trace."

Deacon Harter pointed at the letter on Nancy's table. "If you'd like, I'd be happy to mail it for you tomorrow at the mercantile."

Would he remember to mail it? Her head felt light. Just then, she tried not to fall over. "Sure. That would be thoughtful of you."

He dropped the envelope into his shirt pocket.

At five the summer sun remained high. "Me and Tommy don't need all this food. We'll set plates on the table and let everyone serve themselves. Then we can eat on the porch or at the picnic table. If you can't find a place, you can always sit in the back of your wagons."

A kitchen shelf held a stack of mismatched plates and another stack of saucers. Men ate out of pie pans too. Some folks ate with forks, some with spoons. The spread included fried chicken, deviled eggs, chicken and dumplings, beans, peas, fried okra, sliced tomatoes, pickles, green onions, cornbread, pies, cake, and sweet tea. Nancy hosted a big dinner party and didn't worry about how it went. Where was Amos?

He must have been in trouble. Maybe dead in the woods. She watched her guests pile their plates with fried chicken and caramel cake when a chapter of her life could have closed.

"We can't leave you with this mess to clean up." Peggy Harter scraped and stacked plates. "We'll wash the dishes."

Numb from all the noise of so many people who talked at once and from her heartbreak, Nancy didn't protest. "I'll go to the barn and do the night chores."

Peggy patted Nancy's arm. "You can go out and show the men what has to be done, then come on back inside. Let them do it."

"Yes, ma'am." Whether they'd do everything exactly the way she was used to didn't matter.

"Jimmy," Peggy called. "You men go to the barn and help Sister O'Reilly with the stock."

Soon after the visitors left, Nancy put Tommy to bed without reading to him. He fell asleep during his prayer.

Nancy went to bed too. This day didn't seem real. Amos must have had to stay over and work through the weekend. He'd come home soon.

She'd wake up the next morning with him lying beside her. No, he'd sleep on the porch because he'd come in late. He'd rest outside so he wouldn't want to mess up the bed. He'd need a bath before he slept in the bed.

Tomorrow, while he milked, she'd fry up a mess of ham, scramble six eggs, and make cathead biscuits with tomato gravy. Tommy would help his papa with the chores. Amos would tell her all about what happened to make him late.

She dreamed he came home.

With the first light of day, she looked outside at the porch. Empty. *We have to go to the lumber mill.*

Chapter 4

Four tins with lids behind them waited in a row on the kitchen worktable. Inside each, Nancy placed a molasses cookie and two ham-and-biscuit sandwiches. She added sticks of summer squash and carrots. With her fist she pounded the lids tight.

In his room, Tommy stood by his window and looked out. "Why don't Papa come home?"

"Heaven only knows." She wrung water from a face towel. "Come over here, son."

Hands on his hips and bottom lip stuck out, he stood near the table that held his wash basin. "Do I have to?"

"We're going to the sawmill. You need to look as nice as you did yesterday at church." Nancy scrubbed Tommy's face and left him with a pan of water, bar of soap, and towel. "Wash off and dry. Next put on the clean clothes laid out on your bed."

She went to her bedroom and studied herself in the mirror. Everything looked fine. She could no longer hide the fact she carried a child. Folks would consider it improper for her to go out in public in her condition, but she had little choice.

Tommy marched into her room. "I'm ready, Mama."

"Come let me comb your hair." She dampened it and parted it on the right side. "You've got a cowlick just like your dad's. He has to part his hair on the right too. There. You look sharp."

"Cowlick like Papa's. Blonde hair like yours."

She took the pan of water from his room and sloshed it into the yard from the back porch. From the inside, she latched the back door. "Help me load these lunch pails into the wagon."

He took two of them. "Why you fixed four, Mama?"

She tied on her best bonnet, grabbed her reticule, and picked up the other two lunch pails. "On our way out, let's stop by our new neighbors' place. We can take them lunch."

"When did you load up that jug of water?"

Why did he ask such a question? "Before you woke up this morning."

"Mama, did you know your gun is in the front of the wagon?"

"Yes. I put it there. Don't touch it."

With a skeleton key, she locked the front door, not that it would do any good. "Stay here, Grover. Guard the house." She laid a large hambone in front of him.

"All set." Tommy pulled his body into the wagon.

"Not so fast. Get your hat."

He giggled. "Yes, Mama, but it'll mess up my hair."

"I put the comb in my reticule."

Tommy wrinkled his nose as he fetched his hat.

"Hold on, Tommy." Positioned on the seat of the wagon, she snapped the reins and directed the mule team to the edge of the property. Although the gate stayed open most days, Nancy climbed out of the wagon and closed it.

She turned left on the trail to the Forbess place, where Cleo greeted them with her loud bark. Jeb stood with Evie beside him. Both looked more cleaned up than they did when they arrived at her house two days before.

Jeb removed his hat and ran his fingers through his thick shaggy hair. "Morning, ma'am."

Nancy had cut Amos's hair because of a lack of barbers in their neck of the woods. Who cut Jeb's hair? He could use a trim.

"Good morning." Nancy needed to get on with what she had to say so they could hit the road.

He stood there and grinned. "What brings you in our direction?"

"I packed lunches for Tommy and me, and so I fixed y'all some."

Tommy reached for two of the tins, climbed down, and handed them to Mr. Jeb.

"Mighty nice of you." He took the lunches from Tommy. "Mind if I ask you where y'all are headed so early on this fine morning?"

"To the Mize sawmill."

Jeb raised his palm to her. "Nope, nope, nope."

"What?" Nancy shook her head. "I'll go there if I please. I need to find out what happened to Amos."

"Oh, I heard 'em talking at the mercantile." He turned away from her. "He's gone missing, and you tried to cover it up from me the other day."

"Well, why not?" She clucked to her mules. "We need to go."

"The road to Mize is fraught with danger. No woman and her young son need to be out on the road alone. It ain't that far, but if you have some problems like getting stuck in the mud, you may not come back home till after dark."

"I have to go." There was a cry in her voice.

He lowered his hand and paced on the ground in front of her, then turned to face her. "Now wait just a minute. See this young'un? I done cleaned her up. See these horses? They's hitched to the wagon."

"And?"

"It so happens we was headed to the mill today too. We'll go with you all."

She shook her head. "You were headed to the mill? What for?"

"To order lumber for my house."

She was surprised he had enough money, but she knew so little about the man. "Oh."

"We'll take your mules back to your pasture and hitch my horses to your wagon if that's okay with you."

What would Amos think? This was the most efficient way she had to go look for him. "Well, I suppose that will work."

"Goes without saying. My horses can travel faster than your mules. We can go over to the mill and get back before supper. Your mules may stall out."

"And it rained hard last week." She bit her lip as she thought about the ruts that could be in the road. "We might bog down."

He grinned at her. "Point well taken."

She wished he'd wipe that smirk off his face. "I have to take this risk."

"Give me a second." He loaded Cleo into his wagon and came out with a pistol attached to his belt.

Perched beside Jeb on the wagon seat, Nancy felt foolish for trusting this stranger. What would Amos say? The horses, a magnificent team that moved as though traveling brought them pleasure, took the smooth parts of the road quickly but stepped around the ruts. Tommy and Evie sat cross-legged on quilts spread in the bed of the wagon.

The tall virgin pines on either side of the road filled the air with their woodsy perfume. A breeze whirled through them with the sweet melodies of the small birds of summer adding to the music of nature. Nancy loved riding through the pine forest. Since Amos didn't come home, though, she felt a twinge of guilt as the loveliness of the woods restored serenity within her fretful soul.

"Mr. Jeb." Nancy glanced sideways at him. "I don't even know your last name."

"It's McAllister. Jebediah Leigh McAllister. Jebediah is one of the names King Solomon was known by. It has a special meaning, *beloved of the Lord.* You can call me Jeb."

"Well then, Jeb McAllister, I don't know why I should trust you."

He turned his head toward the children. "It's because I have this darling little girl Evie."

She shook her head. "That fact did influence me, but the main reason is I have to search for Amos."

They traveled in silence along a sandy road, which grew bumpy. Nancy's hands held her belly to keep from jarring the baby.

Jeb slowed his team. "I'm sorry. We don't have to go so fast. Wouldn't want to shake you around too much in your delicate condition."

Nancy's cool hands moved to her face, hot from embarrassment.

"Did I say something wrong?" He shot a glance her way, then turned to look straight ahead. "Hey, I didn't mean nothing. It's improper for me to mention the obvious fact that you're with child."

Her eyes darted toward him for a second before she turned and kept her face aimed at the side of the road to look for signs of Amos and to keep him from seeing her face, which she believed to be red as a ripe plum.

The horses pulled the wagon up a gently rolling hill. She needed to change the subject of the conversation. "This road gets hilly right through here."

"I'm trying to help you find your husband, and yet it goes without mention that I have another man's wife in the wagon on the way to town."

What could she discuss with Mr. Jeb McAllister to ease the stress?

"Where's your wife?"

"At the feet of Jesus." He spoke with confidence. "She was a devout Christian woman."

"Care to talk about it or is it too personal?"

"I can do that. My in-laws, me and my wife and baby girl, and a dozen wagons of folks, most of them related some way or other, headed southwest. We called ourselves the Robinson clan."

She asked, "You came from North Carolina?"

"How'd you know?"

"I hear North Carolina in your accent."

He fixed a tight grin and spoke from the side of his mouth. "Well, ain't you a smart little woman?"

She disliked this man's wiseacre remarks, but she dared not risk letting him know. "I have people from North Carolina."

"Anyway, we headed out. My Mary Ann looked healthy and whole. She was in the family way though and pretty far along." He leaned close to her and almost whispered.

Nancy placed her head within inches of him.

He continued. "The children don't need to hear this. We'd rode a week when she went into labor. Her ma and sister came to help her. She lost the baby and bled out."

Nancy placed a hand on his arm. "So sad."

"We stopped at the nearest town for a funeral and burial. At the end of the day, Mr. Rob, my father-in-law, led us to a place to camp. No turning back."

"What about Evie?"

"My mother-in-law took over little Evie. Things didn't go so well though. They wouldn't let me see her much."

Nancy felt a surge of sympathy for Jeb. "But you got her back. How?"

Chapter 5

Whizz. Zing. A rifle bullet zipped in front of the horses.

Nancy told the children, "Get down and stay flat on your faces. Don't raise your heads."

It took Jeb a few seconds to settle the team. He told Nancy, "Hop out and hide on the north side of the wagon."

She helped Evie jump down.

Tommy followed, keeping as low as he could. The three crouched in a huddle. Jeb knelt beside them and fired his pistol into the air as he held his horses' reins in his left hand. "It's okay, Thunder."

A shout came from the south side of the road. "Hold your fire."

Two men dressed in rags crept from behind bushes. Nancy recognized them as a pair of the bums who threw dice under the big tree next to the mercantile.

"Stay down, y'all." Jeb stood. "What's the sense of shooting at my horses?"

"Howdy, stranger. What's the sense of you riding through the woods with Amos O'Reilly's wife?"

"That would be none of your concern." Jeb helped the children back into the wagon. Nancy resumed her place and raised her shotgun high enough for the attackers to see it.

The taller man slapped his sidekick on the back. "We was just shooting us some lunch."

Jeb shook his head. "This ain't a rabbit month. Don't you know July ain't got an R in it?"

"What we killed for our dinner didn't care none. This here don't know how to spell." The shorter man chuckled as he used a forked stick to lift a dead rattlesnake about four feet long.

The tall one put a dip of snuff in his mouth. "What's the matter? Ain't y'all ever ate fried snake for dinner?"

The short one pulled onto his overalls with his thumbs. "Mister, I don't know what you call yourself doing, but it ain't smart for a stranger to pass through Sullivan's Holler. You's getting awful close to the rim of it. In the holler, we take the law into our own hands."

"Yeah." The taller man hit the short one's arm. "We made one stranger spend the night in a horse stable, and we fed him dried corn for supper. He had to drink out of the horses' watering trough. And the next day…teehee…the next day we hitched him up like a mule and plowed him."

The shorter man spit brown liquid onto the ground. "You think that was something. You got to hear about the time when we killed a man's horse and…"

"That'll be enough. We have a lady here and two little children in the wagon. Show some respect." Jeb held up his pistol. "You call me a stranger, but I own a farm down the road. I suggest you go eat your snake and let us get on with our journey."

"Ain't you got no sense of humor?" The tall man slapped the short one's hat off his head.

Jeb signaled to his horses to move on as he set his jaw in a hard line.

Nancy lowered her shotgun. "It's wise to stay away from the folks from the Hollow for safety's sake."

"They don't bother me none. Men like that bluff their way around."

"You would be shocked at some of the stories about this place."

As they traveled on, Jeb blinked at Nancy. "I suppose you'd like to know what happened causing me to end up with little Evie."

"I would." She glanced around. Tommy and Evie had their eyes closed. "The children didn't worry too much about all that fracas. They must be taking a little snooze. Go ahead and tell me about it."

"I stole her from my mother-in-law."

"The child's grandmother tried to keep her?"

"That's right." Jeb bit his lip and stared ahead. "You might say Old Man Robinson despised me and blamed me for what happened to Mary Ann. He tried to run me out of the traveling band. I asked to take my little girl back and let her ride in my wagon.

"'No,' she said. 'It ain't safe.' I'd be busy watching the horses and she'd fall out. Besides, a man wouldn't know how to take care of a little girl."

"You love her." Nancy's eyes shone. "I can see you do."

"She's all I have left of Mary Ann."

As they rode on, Nancy looked for any signs of Amos.

Jeb continued his story. "We was crossing Tennessee, and the Robinsons bought some corn whiskey. Most everybody got drunk, but I didn't. My in-laws just about passed out. I grabbed up Evie and left with her. Nobody came looking for the child. They probably believed she wandered off and drowned or something worse. I turned left and headed to the hill country of Mississippi."

At the mill, Jeb arranged to buy the lumber to build his house.

Nancy asked the foreman about Amos. "Did he leave on Friday at the usual time?"

"He did. And come Monday, he didn't show up for work."

On the way home, they passed through a little community, consisting of five houses, and ate lunch under a large oak tree.

As they resumed the trip home, Nancy looked for Amos all along the road.

Evie pulled on the back of Jeb's shirt. "Sing, Papa."

Jeb looked at Nancy. "While we travel, we sing. It helps. Do you mind?"

"No, go ahead." Nancy kept looking at the side of the road for Amos.

He led a rousing rendition of "Old MacDonald Had a Farm."

Evie and Tommy joined in. The gloom dissolved and all their moods lifted. Nancy didn't think it would be appropriate for her to sing with Jeb. She made a faint smile as she looked from one side of the road to the other for some clue of what could have happened to Amos.

"Oh, come on, Miss Nancy." Jeb caught his breath while the children kept going with the animal noises. "It won't hurt to make life fun for the children."

"You're right." Nancy joined in.

They sang the alphabet song.

Jeb sang "Home on the Range."

"Nice." Nancy made a sad smile.

"Sing with me."

She blended with him in soft alto harmony.

Jeb held the horses to a slow gait on the way home.

When they reached Nancy's house, she was exhausted. "Hello, Grover. We're glad to see you. Go to the barn with me while I milk. Then me and Tommy will feed the chickens, mules, and hogs."

Jeb held sleepy Evie in his arms. "It's the only neighborly thing to do. I'll milk."

Nancy turned the covers back on her bed. "Lay her down here. I'll wash her off."

Jeb tousled Tommy's hair. "Son, do you feel like helping feed?"

Such a kind man.

While Jeb and Tommy did the barn chores, Nancy whipped up some hoecakes.

Evie bounced off the bed. "I'm hungry, Miss Nancy."

Jeb and Tommy washed their hands and the two families sat at the table with a lighted lamp in the middle. Jeb said grace.

After they ate, Nancy handed a bottle of milk to Jeb. "Take this with you."

As soon as Jeb and Evie left, she cleaned the kitchen while Tommy readied himself for bed. After his prayers, she went to bed exhausted.

Lord, help us find Amos. Keep Tommy and me safe. The only protection I have is our precious dog Grover and my shotgun. Nobody's going to get past Grover. I will trust in you. And one more thing, bless our new neighbors. In Jesus' name.

Her father was still alive, and so was Granny. Her other three grandparents had passed away before she was born. Granny had told her so many stories about them that it felt as though she knew them. Her mother had died when Nancy was six years old. She saw them in her sleeping visions. That night after she drifted off, she dreamed about her childhood.

After a few hours of hard sleep, her eyes popped open. She lay awake, rigid with anger boiling within. Amos wasn't coming back. *Why?* At that moment, the reality that he had truly disappeared permeated her mind. She couldn't stop her anxiety. She'd never done anything to hurt anybody. She'd tried to teach her son to love God. She'd been the best wife she knew how to be. Was this what she deserved? It was worse than being a widow.

It was time for her to decide what to do. She tried to organize her life.

She should go back home near Port Gibson, but how? Her new neighbor Jeb must have money. He paid cash for a large pile of lumber. Would he like to buy her mules, wagon, cows, chickens, and pigs? Maybe he'd buy the house and farm.

What if her father refused to let her move into his home? He had not given her his blessings when she married Amos. It would take weeks to tend to all her business, and Jeb might not want her farm. She knew what her father would say. She'd heard him make insensitive remarks about other young women when they married. He would tell Nancy, "You've made your bed hard. Now lie in it."

But, Pa, I could help take care of you and Grandma. Wouldn't you love having the children near?

He'd written her a letter saying that he'd lost everything he had in the war and had little hope of recovering.

She'd offered him and Granny to come live with her, but he wrote her back that he didn't take charity, especially from his daughter.

Again she prayed. *Dear Lord, I will trust in you. Thank you, Father, for the angels who watch over us.*

All she had was the farm with its livestock.

Better get some rest. We'll harvest corn tomorrow.

Chapter 6

O God, if you'll keep us from evil, I promise to bring this baby I'm carrying and my son up to honor you. They're all I have. I give them to you.

While the sky enclosed the farm in gray Tuesday morning, Nancy milked. They finished the chores and hitched the mules to the wagon.

On the shelf lay tattered gloves. "I'm sorry, Tommy. I ordered some new gloves from the catalogue, but they haven't come in the mail yet. The mercantile doesn't have any."

As they rode to the field, she prayed. *If you'll bring Amos home, I'll do my best to be a better wife and mother.*

As she busied her hands harvesting the corn with Tommy's help, she turned her heart to prayer.

Show me, dear Lord, where I have sinned. Please forgive my selfish ways.

Nancy parked the wagon by the field, and Tommy walked with her to take the mules back to their pasture. They returned to the rows by the wagon, where they made slow progress harvesting the dried corn ears.

The sharp corn husks made her hands bleed. Blisters formed, but she didn't stop working. What hurt even more was that Tommy's young skin cracked and blistered too. The child's back bent over as he tried to carry a man's load of their precious harvest.

"Mama." Tommy, with blood on his shirt, threw the ears he'd plucked into the wagon.

Her heart ached. "Yes?"

"We're harvesting this corn in earnest, ain't we?"

She suppressed her chuckle. *In earnest* sounded too adult for a six-year-old. So much to do on the farm. She loved the smell of the dried corn ears. They'd have the job of throwing the corn into the crib. She breathed a heavy sigh. How could she find the strength to cut the stalks and stack them like teepees for the cows to eat later?

"Tommy, you want to know something good?"

"What, Mama?"

"Your Papa's done laid the cotton by. Saturday before last, he finished plowing the middles deep to turn the dirt onto the rows. All we have to do is watch it grow and pray it gets the right amount of rain."

And the watermelons. What was she going to do with all those watermelons? Amos's melons ripened later than his neighbors', and they tasted sweeter. Since the crop was late and the competition was dwindling, they would bring a good price if they hauled them in the wagon to a spot near the mercantile. How would she lift them, especially the larger ones?

Tuesday and Wednesday, Nancy and Tommy worked as hard as they could. Her hands hurt, but she ignored sore hands. Thursday morning, they started the day as they had the two previous ones, but a powerful wind brought in dark clouds. Nancy stopped at midmorning and took what they'd gathered to the crib. All afternoon, the rain poured in the midst of thunder and lightning.

While Tommy played, Nancy sewed, careful not to spill blood from her cracked hands. She had enough projects to keep her busy if she did nothing else but sew. Tommy needed clothes for school. She planned to cut shirts and trousers from Amos's old clothes. She should make clothes for the baby, and it would be fun to make a dress for little Evie. She decided to make the dress that day.

Friday, the rain fell. On a shelf in her room were folded pieces of fabric, mostly remnants, for her to sew. She included clothes that she and Amos had worn until they were no longer useful. It was possible to cut away the threadbare parts of garments so she could use the good cloth for children's clothing or quilts. She never wasted anything.

As the day passed, she examined the fabrics, mostly old clothes. What would make a good shirt for Tommy to wear to school?

Another Friday evening passed without Amos's return.

When Nancy and Tommy went to the barn, they wore boots. The rain soaked their bodies as they performed their chores.

How must it have been for Jeb to be confined in his little wagon house with Evie? They couldn't cook outside because of the rain. It would have been neighborly to invite them over to spend the evening inside her cozy house, but it seemed inappropriate.

How would it have gone over if Amos had returned that night from wherever he was? What if Amos had walked through the front door of his house and found Nancy entertaining another man? Would he understand that Jeb was like a brother?

She and Jeb were two lonely souls, each trying to bring up a child. She found Jeb a kindred spirit. He was in her mind the big brother she never had. She knew she had to guard her heart, had to be careful not to do anything unseemly.

Saturday, the sun shone bright, but the middles between the corn rows held water. Nancy kept busy sewing and tried to still the storms within her mind.

At night she tossed in her feather bed. In her dreams of Amos, she talked to him. *I will always love you. I pray every night you are safe. All day long, I think of you.*

She coaxed the mules to pull the wagon up the saturated red clay hill to church Sunday. They slid to the edge. *Lord, please don't let us slide in the ditch. Don't let us turn over.*

Tommy cried. "Oh, no."

She managed to steer the mules back to the center of the road.

In the worship service, Deacon Harter asked if anybody had any prayer needs. Trembling with embarrassment to voice a complaint in her life and thinking that as a woman she shouldn't speak in the congregational assembly, Nancy stood and held onto the back of the pew in front of her. "Pray that me and my boy Tommy can harvest our corn. We try hard, but we don't make much progress. I don't mean to whine. We are truly blessed."

Several members spoke at once. Deacon Harter gained their attention. "This Wednesday, we'll go to Sister O'Reilly's house and help her out of her troubles. Menfolk and womenfolk and children can all come. The men can work in Brother Amos's fields. The women can bring dinner and assist Miss Nancy with sewing and quilting and the like."

All Her Dreams of Love

After church, the Harters came to her wagon. Peggy Harter hugged Nancy. "Y'all come to our house for Sunday dinner."

Nancy bit her lip. "That would be imposing. Besides I've got to figure out how to drive down that hill to go home."

Harold Harter stepped closer and raised his hand. "It ain't safe. I don't know how you got up it. You can go home on the back road that goes through our farm. After dinner, I'll show you the way."

Wednesday developed into a festive occasion. Jeb McAllister came by. Perhaps he heard all the commotion. He left Evie at the O'Reilly house with the women while he helped harvest the corn. They stacked the ripe watermelons by a tree in Nancy's front yard. The neighbors ate dinner on the porch and the backs of the wagons with Nancy providing watermelon for all.

Jeb stood by the porch to eat with Evie. The Harters sat nearby. Nancy opened the conversation. "Deacon, did you know that Mr. Jeb here has plans to build a fine house at the old Forbess place?"

Deacon laid his fried drumstick on his plate. "Oh, really?"

"Yes." Jeb beamed. "As soon as the lumber gets delivered, I hope to frame it. Right now, I'm working on the foundation."

"When you get your lumber, we'll have a house raising for you if you'd like."

"I would." When Jeb smiled, his teeth gleamed like pearls.

The men shook hands.

"I have hooks in the ceiling and a quilting frame." Nancy pointed toward her front door. Amos had been considerate to mount the hooks for her. "The women can come help me quilt."

Peggy raised an eyebrow. "The women in the neighborhood could start a quilting club."

The deacon turned toward Jeb. "You and the little one are welcome to come to church."

"Thank you."

The men went back to the field. The women cleaned the kitchen and returned to their sewing projects.

After Evie's nap, Nancy gave her a bath on the back porch. By the end of the afternoon, Evie had four new dresses.

"Have any of you talked to the midwife lately?" Nancy rubbed her tired back. "Has she been seen in our neck of the woods? I've got four more months to go, but I'd like to let her know about my expected date of confinement."

Chapter 7

Dinner on the grounds at church came around often. It was a good way to make sure Pastor Barlow and his wife and children shared a tasty meal with the congregation. When the time came for desserts, the members of each family shifted into separate groups - the men stood around a tree on the far edge of the church property, the older children sneaked away from their parents, and the women stayed close enough to supervise the children and guard their food.

With Tommy and Evie holding molasses teacakes as they strolled beside her, Nancy drifted over to the other women with small children. She held a bowl of pear cobbler covered with a crust rich with butter and sugar. "Jenny Mae, this cobbler is perfect. I've been craving me some good cobbler."

Jenny Mae Bynum stood taller.

Peggy Harter placed a gentle hand on Nancy's belly. "You still looking for a midwife?"

Nancy broke off a piece of crust. "Yes. When Tommy was born, old Mrs. May delivered him."

"But she passed away." Peggy rested the side of her head in her hand. "A midwife all the way from Raleigh comes through here when somebody gets in touch with her, but she tries to see about women over too big a territory."

Nancy eased Peggy's hand away. "It must be hard to catch up with her, but it's worth a try."

"Birthing babies ain't no big deal. Somebody just has to catch the baby and tie off the cord if everything goes right. Except sometimes it don't." Jenny Mae looked deep into Nancy's eyes. "I'm sorry. I shouldn't have said that. You know what I mean though. We'll pray everything goes well with you."

Tommy tugged on Nancy's hand and pointed to a group of children nearby. "Mommy, can I play over there?"

"Sure. Go ahead."

"It must be awful going through this without Amos." Jenny Mae ruined the taste of the cobbler.

Nancy stuck out her chin. "The Lord's going to see me through."

Women gathered their leftovers, which they loaded into their wagons and surreys. Most of them used bed sheets for tablecloths. These they laid over the food to keep away the flies.

Nancy dawdled. She and Tommy had ridden to church with Jeb and little Evie in his new surrey. She wanted to wait until the women with wagging tongues like Josephine and her cronies drove away.

Nothing inappropriate was going on. As a neighborly gesture, Jeb had given her a ride to church. She was having more trouble hitching up the mules because her belly got in the way.

Jeb must have felt a little discomfort, too, because he waited until the crowd thinned to come over and help her load up.

"Jeb, this is a fine surrey you bought." She blew a strand of hair out of her face.

He spoke in a soft voice. "I got a good deal on it."

He didn't brag, but he showed evidence of financial comfort. After buying all that lumber, he bought a wagon and a pair of mules. Next, a surrey.

Too bad Amos couldn't be here to enjoy living next to Jeb, who had neighborly ways. The two men would have enjoyed one another's company.

Midmorning, while Tommy shelled field peas, Nancy busied herself with kitchen chores. Her back ached down low. It would feel good to sit a spell. Churn some butter.

As she finished the job, somebody knocked on the floor of her porch near the edge. B. K. never stepped onto her porch to knock at her door. The pattern sounded like B. K. Grover didn't bark.

"Miss Nancy," he called.

Nancy rose and placed a hand on her back, then walked outside onto the porch. "Good morning, B. K."

He removed his hat. "Yes'm. Good morning. It sure is."

"What brings you our way?" When Nancy heard commotion behind her, she looked around.

Tommy stood inside, where he looked out the window.

"Come on outside, Tommy."

B. K. stared at the ground a moment before looking up. "Me and Bertie be needing fresh milk. Our cow's done gone dry."

Nancy didn't hesitate. "I can spare you some."

"We ain't got no money, but I bet you could stand to have your stables cleaned out."

One more job Nancy couldn't do. *Thank you, Lord.* "Yes. And the manure spread over the field."

"I can work till dinner time about noon, and you can give me a molasses can of milk. Is that a deal?"

Nancy couldn't help smiling. She'd also include some fresh butter and a mess of peas. "Deal!"

B. K.'s sons, Arnold and Matthew, pushed each other into a clear spot from the other side of a bush, where they had been hiding.

"Come on out here, boys. Stop acting like you ain't got good sense." He turned toward Nancy. "They don't never go around nobody."

Nancy chuckled. "Tommy, come say hello to Arnold and Matthew."

Tommy stepped forward and held up his hand in a wave. "Howdy."

Arnold and Matthew waved.

"How old are you?" Nancy asked.

B. K. spoke for them. "They's eight and nine. Both of them's good workers. They're going to help me."

"When y'all finish working, come back and pick you out a couple of watermelons. You can have any you want, but you don't want to pick some that are too heavy to tote all the way back to your house."

"Much obliged." B. K. picked up his stained hat from the porch floor and shoved it down tight on his head. "Come on, boys. Let's get to work."

After they finished, Nancy handed B. K. two pails. "This one's sweet milk, and here's some buttermilk."

"Much obliged."

"Hold on a minute." She handed him a little sack with a jar inside it. "Here's some fresh butter. I churned it this morning."

Arnold reached for it.

"Here, Matthew. This is a sack of fresh field peas y'all can have for supper."

The next morning, Nancy sat peeling pears on the porch while Tommy shelled more peas.

Tommy hurled hulls into a bucket. "We'll never quit shelling peas."

"Son, just be glad we've got all these peas. We'll enjoy eating them fresh, and this winter we'll be glad to have dry peas."

Jeb drove up to her porch in the surrey. Evie, wearing one of her pretty new dresses, sat beside him. He pulled back the reins. "Whoa."

She laid down her knife. "Good morning."

"What's going on? Either Amos has come home or you're out of your mind."

Nancy shook her head. "I've been praying hard that Amos is all right and that he would come home, but who knows what happened to him?"

Jeb looked at the ground. "I'm sorry. I shouldn't have said that."

She resumed peeling pears. "That I'm out of my head? What made you say such a thing?"

Jeb pointed behind him. "How did you get all that manure dumped into the cornfield?"

She smiled. "I didn't do it for sure. Have you met B. K. Barnes?"

"Can't say as I have. Who is that?"

"B. K. is a freedman. Him and his wife Bertie and their two boys and a little girl live in a log cabin near the creek. They have a forty-acre farm. It's good land, except when the Cohay floods. Thank goodness their cabin is on stilts."

"And he did all that work for you?"

"Yes. His cow has dried up, and he needed milk. He was ashamed to ask me."

"Oh, I get it. He worked for you."

"Right. I traded milk, butter, and watermelons for him cleaning out some of the stables. I don't think I paid him enough."

"Do you need anything from the mercantile? Me and Evie are headed over there. Or maybe you and Tommy would like to go."

Nancy looked into the distance. Would people get the wrong idea? "Well, I don't know."

Tommy put down his dishpan of peas. "Please, Mama."

"Well, okay." She stood. "Let's set our stuff inside. Give us a minute to get ready."

Nancy still had money saved back. In addition to the regular food supplies, she bought a few links of fabric and spools of thread. As Felton Oglethorpe helped her select thread to match the fabric, she noticed his white hands. The cloying aroma of an excess of bay rum mixed with the smell of sweat nauseated her. She backed away, and he stepped closer.

As they rode back to her house, Jeb asked her, "What do you plan to do with all that cloth?"

"Many things."

The next time B. K. came to see Nancy, he brought his entire family. Bertie held their little girl, a toddler, Cora Lee, about two years old. "I came to see if you had any work for me to do. You being in the family way and your husband missing."

"The news gets around." Nancy placed her hands on her belly. "I can't hide the obvious."

Bertie blinked her large brown eyes. "I didn't mean nothing ugly."

"Let me see if we can make a deal. Would you mind washing our clothes and sheets and putting fresh sheets on the beds?"

Bertie nodded. "Yes'm. I can do that."

"While you're doing that, I'll make you a new dress."

Bertie's eyes flashed. "You got material to spare?"

"Come on in here." Nancy led the way to the kitchen table, where the new fabric lay in a stack. "Select the piece you want, and I'll sew on your dress while you work."

Girl-like, Bertie examined each piece of fabric. She held up the bright blue piece that had yellow flowers scattered throughout. "I like this one."

"Okay." Nancy brought out her tape measure. "Let me stretch this around you in a few places."

While Nancy worked, Bertie chatted. "Me and my family and you and your boy's going to be hungry come dinner time.

If it don't matter to you, I could cook some of them peas and make some cornbread."

Nancy wrote some measurements on a scrap of paper. "That would be very good. And we could have tomatoes, onions, and peppers from the garden."

"Don't think I want to eat inside your fine house. If'n we did, sure as shooting, some white man would show up here. If they caught us eating at your table, they'd burn your house down and our cabin too. Besides, them men folk going to smell awful after cleaning barn stables all morning. We can eat in the yard."

Nancy folded up her tape. "Me and Tommy can eat on the porch."

In the middle of the afternoon, Bertie tried on her dress. "It's pretty, and it fits me."

Nancy turned up a section of the bottom and pinned it. "I'll need to hem it."

Bertie changed back into her old dress. "If'n you ain't too tired sewing, I'll get them menfolks to help take care of the stock, and I'll do the milking."

"Oh, good. Tommy can show you how we do our barn chores, can't you, son?"

The boy beamed with a look of pride. "Yes, ma'am."

Nancy didn't look up from her sewing project. "Before that, Bertie, why don't you go pick a mess of peas?"

Bertie found a bucket. "Now, let me ask you something. I know there ain't no white women around here delivering babies. I done delivered more colored babies than I can count. Would you be willing for me to help you have your baby?"

"Bertie, if you only knew how much I've pondered over this problem. My baby is due around late November or early December. I'd love for you to help me."

Chapter 8

"How am I supposed to do this?" The baby made it impossible for Nancy to sit on the stool. When she tried to squat onto it, she lost her balance. Her large abdomen got in the way. *I have to milk, but I can't figure out a way to do it.*

To keep from falling, she spread her legs as far apart as she could tolerate. *Oh, this is miserable.* Bending over to squeeze the cow's teats placed her back in a bind.

Old Flossie cow must have sensed something unnatural was going on. At the moment Nancy propped the bucket against the stool, Flossie brought her foot forward and caused Nancy to spill part of the milk she'd worked hard to acquire.

One down and one to go. She straightened and rubbed her back.

Bella, the second cow misbehaved also. They sensed her awkwardness, she supposed. When she finished, she stretched her back. Toting the heavy pail, she held onto the edge of the stall so she wouldn't fall. Milking two cows was enough work to set up a backache that would last all morning.

Nancy was glad Bertie came over in the late afternoons to milk and take two molasses tins of the fresh nourishment to her children. When Bertie came to do the laundry after a week had passed, Nancy pulled out the remnant leftover from

Bertie's dress. "I'll make Cora Lee one like yours. Would it be too much trouble to run home and get one of the little girl's dresses so I can use it for a pattern?"

"No'm." Bertie turned around and started running down the hill toward her cabin. "I'll be right back."

As B. K. and his sons finished mucking the stables and spreading the manure, Jeb showed up. "I'd like to hire you and your boys to help work on my house."

B. K. shook his head and rubbed the back of his neck. "I ain't no carpenter."

"That's all right. Y'all can clean up the yard. I'll show you how to hold boards for me."

Sunday morning on the way to church, Jeb helped Nancy into the surrey, and she piled up next to him. The children sat on the back seat. "You don't seem to get around so well these days. What's the hardest job you have?"

"Milking."

"Two cows twice a day."

"Yes." She cooled her hot face with her fan. "Most evenings, Bertie Barnes takes care of the chore. I share the milk with her. I still have more than I can use for butter and cottage cheese."

"I could do it in the mornings. Could you share some milk with Evie and me?"

"Deal." She nodded with enthusiasm. "Bring Evie by and I'll watch her. If you want me to, I'll keep her all day while you work on your house."

"You sure?" He placed his hat on the seat between them. "I'm always afraid she'll get hurt around the construction. You would be a big help."

"She's no trouble."

As they rode along, Nancy stared into the woods. Most nights, she dreamed that Amos returned. It didn't make sense for her to think he'd appear out of nowhere, but she couldn't stop her feelings.

In her front yard, the pile of watermelons next to the tall tree remained, although it had diminished. Jeb pointed toward the pile. "You had any watermelon lately?"

"No, me and Tommy have grown tired of them. I gave some to the Barnes children a while back."

"I suspect they're past their prime."

She brought her hand to her mouth. "Oh, no. I wouldn't want to give anybody spoiled food."

He chuckled. "The pigs will eat them, though. Why don't I give them some watermelon every morning?"

"Great idea."

In the middle of a hot afternoon, Jeb showed up for no announced reason and hitched Nancy's mules to her wagon.

"Let's go for a ride." They drove through Amos and Nancy's cotton fields. Occasional yellowish-white blooms showed up scattered through the dark green leaves.

"Look. Papa." Evie pointed. "Flowers...pretty."

"Yes, sweetheart." Jeb reached an arm around Evie, who was standing up behind him and Nancy. "Starting to bloom. In a few weeks you'll have cotton."

"Right. The yellow blooms will be everywhere. It's a beautiful sight. Then they turn a shade of deep pink." Nancy didn't know how she'd harvest the cotton. She wrung her hands. "It looks like Amos is going to have a big yield this year."

Jeb gazed across the fields. "Three or four bales."

He jumped down from the wagon and picked two blooms, which he presented to Nancy and Evie. "Flowers for the ladies."

Nancy cupped the delicate bloom in her hands. "Thank you."

Jeb's voice dropped to a low, melancholy tone. "If Amos were here, I'm sure he would have given you a blossom."

Tommy hugged his mother. "I can help pick cotton, Mama."

They rode down to the Barneses' cabin. Jeb shook his head. "B. K. settled too close to the creek."

Nancy dipped her head forward. "This is the only land the government would give him. He claimed forty acres to homestead here, but they ran out of surplus mules years ago. Bertie told me he was excited to get this rich soil to farm. He knew floods might come sometimes, but he didn't think he had a choice. They'd spent years moving from one place to another, and they were sick of sharecropping."

The Barneses' cotton field lay between their cabin and the creek. It was already covered with pink blooms.

"His cotton is way ahead of yours."

For the next few weeks, the O'Reillys, the McAllisters, and the Barneses continued to survive. Too bad Amos couldn't see how the three families thrived as they helped one another. In the middle of the night, she heard noises outside, sounds that awakened her from her dreams about her precious husband who still had not come home. Grover's barks drew her to the front room window.

The moon shone bright, and she saw the raccoons. The panther that roamed through the Cohay Creek swamps cried out like a woman in pain. Bobcats mewed in the trees, owls whooed, and whippoorwills called. The music of the night she'd heard all the years she'd lived near Cohay came to her from all directions, but none of it frightened her. It was the life she'd come to know.

August moved along with its intense heat until the winds of September brought some cooler, more restful evenings.

As a meditation before bedtime, she read, "Casting all your care upon him; for he careth for you." (1 Peter 5:7 KJV)

Lord, it's only a few days till Tommy starts school. He's ready for first grade. Thank you for such a smart little man. I want to walk him to school. It's way too far for him to go alone. It's getting more difficult for me to traipse through the woods. How can I get him there? Thank you for this intelligent child. It would be unfortunate to hold him back a year.

Sweet sleep with lovely dreams kept her comfortable until the sun rose.

Monday midmorning, Tommy ran into the house. "Mama, our pigs is gone. They done broke out of their pen."

Nancy picked up Evie. "Come on, children. We've got to get help."

They'd broken loose last spring. Amos had planned to build them new pens, but he reinforced the old ones with the hope they'd stay there until he had time. When they got loose, they turned into monsters.

"Come on." She sprinted toward Jeb's house, but after a few breaths, she slowed down.

"I went to check on them." Tommy ran along and talked until he needed to breathe.

"Come on, Tommy."

"They was gone," Tommy shouted.

"Little girl, I can't carry you any farther." She let Evie down to the ground. "Walk as fast as you can."

When they got within sight of Jeb's house, Nancy told Tommy, "Run on ahead. Tell the men to come quick."

Tommy ran to the house and returned with Jeb, B. K., and the Barnes brothers.

Jeb arrived first and picked up Evie. "What's wrong?"

Nancy talked through a sigh. "The pigs broke out of their pen."

All seven people marched toward Nancy's house. Jeb asked, "Any idea where they might be?"

"Most likely they went to the hickor' nut tree." Nancy, out of breath, tried to keep up. "I'm sorry to interfere with y'all's work."

"It's okay." Jeb turned around and waited for her to catch up. "You did the right thing."

B. K. laughed. "Pigs loves hickor' nuts."

A dark cloud came over Jeb's eyes. "Why don't you take Evie and go back home? We can handle this."

"No," she insisted. "I need to show you where the hickor' nut tree is."

"Where, Miss Nancy?" B. K. asked.

"Up at the top of this little hill." The pasture lay on an upward incline. Nancy puffed as she climbed the rolling incline. Underneath the tree next to the fence on the far side, the boar and two sows with piglets rooted at a furious pace.

Jeb handed Evie to Nancy. "Watch out. Don't get in front of them."

The boar grunted as it stormed toward Jeb, but Jeb threw a nut, which hit the animal between his eyes. "Get on back home."

A sow charged toward B. K. and with her snout grabbed the leg of his overalls. B. K. tripped and fell. The sow rooted at him, and he curled into a ball while Grover and Cleopatra chased the sow away.

Nancy rushed over to B. K. "Are you all right?"

He brushed himself off. "Yeah, that was a close call."

"Your leg's bleeding."

B. K. pushed himself up from the ground. "I hit a rock when I fell."

"Your overalls are torn," Nancy said.

The old hog turned and ran toward his stall with the others following.

Jeb ripped off his shirt and tied it around B.K.'s. leg.

Nancy looked the other way, as she forced herself not to gaze at Jeb's manly shoulders covered only by the straps of his overalls.

The pigs ran to their pen. Jeb laughed. "I suppose they remember I'm the one who fed them watermelons. Pigs are smart that way."

She demanded B. K. allow her to help him. "Come to the house. I need to see about your leg."

B. K. with his boys went to her back porch. Tommy and Evie followed along. When they reached the porch, she told B. K.'s sons, Tommy, and Evie to go stay on the front porch. "Tommy, keep an eye on Evie."

She washed his leg and applied a tight dressing of white rags to stop the bleeding.

"Wait here a minute, B. K."

"I need to go help Mr. Jeb."

"No, you must not go near the hog pens. If you get manure in this wound, you might end up with lockjaw." She went inside and found a pair of Amos's overalls. "Wait here a minute."

"Yes, ma'am."

"I'm going around to the front of the house." She handed him the overalls. "They look like they'll fit you, but you will have to roll up the pants in big cuffs. You and Amos are about the same size, except he's taller."

He took the overalls with a smile. "Thank you, Miss Nancy."

"Give me time to get to the front porch. Then change your clothes."

When they returned from taking care of the pigs, men were stealing lumber. Jeb shot into the air. The thieves dropped the lumber and ran.

"Cleo, it's too bad you and Grover can't be more than one place at a time."

The first Sunday of September on the way to church, Nancy sat on the bouncing seat of the surrey. Although she had turned her problem of helping Tommy go to school over to the Lord, she'd taken it back.

"What's on your mind?"

She told Jeb that Tommy would start school come Monday morning.

"I think I know where the schoolhouse is." Jeb frowned. "It's on a rough road over toward Steve Bynum's house. I visited him the other day when my horse Thunder threw a shoe."

"Right. I plan to walk with him there because the road is too bad to take him in the wagon." She clutched her belly. "Besides, it's done got hard for me to hitch up the mules."

"Mrs. O'Reilly, I'd be honored to take Tommy to school. After we do the morning chores, I'll give him a ride. On pretty days, I might walk with him. Your help with Evie leaves me obligated to you."

"Aww." *Lord, thank you for providing such a caring neighbor when I needed one.*

After Sunday lunch, Nancy and Tommy relaxed on the front porch. Despite all she had going on, Nancy felt an obligation to spend some peaceful time on Sunday afternoon as a token observance of the Sabbath.

While Tommy sat holding a McGuffey reader Amos had passed down to him, Nancy sat with her needlework. She let her hands go limp as she released all the tension in her body.

Grover barked with the sound he made when a stranger approached. Nancy bolted from her chair. Amos?

No.

She went back to sit again as Felton Oglethorpe arrived in his wagon. "Son, don't move out of your seat."

"What's going on, Mama?"

"Oh, nothing."

Mr. Oglethorpe pulled up to the parking place in front of the porch and stopped his mule team. He nodded forward as he tipped his hat. "Good afternoon, Mrs. O'Reilly."

She made her voice sound as flat as she could. "Good evening."

"Howdy, Tommy."

Tommy raised his hand with the wave he used for a greeting.

It was the first time she'd seen Oglethorpe wearing overalls and a work shirt. "What brings you out this Sunday afternoon?"

"Amos told me a while ago you'd sell me a couple of shoats." He motioned with his head at two crates in the wagon. "Thought they were about ready to wean. You could use the money, I'm sure. with Amos missing."

"It's the Lord's Day."

"Sunday's the only day I've got to come get the pigs."

She tightened her mouth and nodded. "I see. You'll need help catching 'em. Don't look to me and Tommy."

"B. K. and his boys are going to meet me here in a few minutes."

Lord, please watch over B. K. I pray his wound is closed up.

Chapter 9

When Monday morning came, Nancy's heart overflowed with a mixture of feelings. She'd prepared Tommy for the moment when he would step away from her into his new beginning. If only she could replay the six years when her child was all hers...how she wished she could have Amos here sharing this milestone.

On the front porch an hour earlier than usual, Tommy stood dressed in the shirt he'd worn the day before. "Good morning, Mama."

She went over to him and gave him a quick hug. "Whatcha doing?"

"Getting dressed to help with the chores. I didn't want to mess up my school clothes."

"How considerate!"

Tommy scratched the dog's neck. "Come on, Grover."

"Not much to do. Bertie will come milk soon. I'll collect the eggs later."

After breakfast, Tommy brushed his teeth long and hard with his sweetgum brush.

"You can stop now, son." Nancy noticed a pink tinge when he spit out the baking soda.

After Nancy scrubbed his ears and neck with a coarse face towel and lye soap, she parted his hair. "Don't be messing with it."

He buttoned up his starched white shirt and fastened his overalls.

"Tomorrow, you may want to wear your short pants, but on the first day, you need to wear long ones. Let me know what the other boys wear."

"Okay." His eyes froze in a gaze at nothing in particular. Whatever he felt, he didn't let her know. He was already becoming his own person.

Nancy tucked wisps of hair inside her Sunday bonnet. She wanted to look her best on Tommy's first day of school.

He pulled on his socks, pushed his feet into his brogans, pulled the laces tight, and tied his shoes.

"I'm proud of you for learning to tie your shoes."

When he finished, he stuck his thumb and a finger inside his mouth and wiggled. "Mama, I've got a loose tooth."

"Don't fool with it. You don't want it to fall out and bleed on your school clothes. When you come home after school and take off your best shirt, you can work on it then."

"Let's wait on the porch, Mama." Holding his slate, Tommy rushed out the front door.

Nancy recorded a picture in her mind as her son stood on the steps. She'd cherish the moment forever.

Jeb pulled the surrey up to the edge of the porch, lifted Evie into the back seat, and helped Nancy climb in. Tommy sat tall.

How difficult was it for Jeb to starch and iron a shirt? "You've made a special effort to look nice this morning."

"So have you." He flashed a broad smile that showed his white teeth.

Evie spread the skirt of her dress. "Look at me."

"What a pretty dress!" Nancy reached an outstretched hand toward the little girl.

The surrey bounced over the deep ruts cut into it during the rains. Next to the open door of the log schoolhouse stood a petite young woman, less than five feet tall. Her dark brown hair hung in a single braid down her back.

"There's the teacher." Jeb threw his head back. "When Deacon Harter introduced her yesterday, I couldn't believe she looked so young."

"Somebody said she's twenty, but you'd think she was a child because she's tiny." Nancy watched to see whether Jeb ogled her. Shame welled within her because she felt jealous. She had no right. It was just that Jeb had become a good friend. She still grieved for Amos, who would come home to her any day. What was she thinking? That Jeb didn't' need to fall for someone who wasn't worthy of him. Also, he needed to spend more time mourning for Mary Ann.

Nancy helped Tommy prepare for his second day at school. *Time to adjust to a new routine.* Jeb left Evie to spend the day and took Tommy, now missing a front tooth, to school.

"If you don't mind, Bertie, gather the eggs. Divide them into threes. I'll give some to Jeb and Evie and keep some for us. You take the rest."

Bertie didn't smile. "Yes, ma'am."

"You seem glum today." *Not that Bertie has to look pleasant all the time, no matter what, like she did before she was set free, but something has upset her.*

Bertie turned around to face Nancy. "It ain't right."

All sorts of things weren't right. "What's that?"

Tears slipped from Bertie's eyes. "My boys deserve to learn they letters. They ain't slaves."

"You're right. I'm sorry they can't go to school." Nancy sighed. "If you'll bring them with you every morning, I'll teach them to read and write."

"Would you do that, Miss Nancy?"

"I said I would."

Wednesday after Jeb took Tommy to school and Bertie went to the barn, Arnold and Matthew Barnes sat on the floor of Nancy's front porch. Barefoot and dressed in their work overalls and shirts, they whispered to each other.

Nancy came outside holding Evie's hand. "Sweet girl, you can play in the sand pile."

Evie descended the steps. In the sand, she grabbed the bucket and a big spoon.

"Good morning, Arnold and Matthew. Come sit up here in these chairs on the porch."

They stood. Arnold frowned. "Miss Nancy, is you sure it's all right for me and Matthew to sit on your porch?"

"I invited you." She shook her head. "Come on. We've got schoolwork to do."

She passed a slate to each boy and kept one. Also, she handed them rags and pieces of chalk.

"Watch my hand and make every move the same way I do." She wrote the letter *A* on her slate.

The lesson continued with more letters. It lasted an hour with Bertie watching from behind them when she finished her chores. She stood and patted their shoulders. "Go on, boys. Your pa and Mr. Jeb's already a-working. I heard hammering."

"Yes, Mama."

"Mind your manners," Bertie said.

Arnold looked up. "Thanks, Miss Nancy."

"It was my pleasure." Nancy stood to stretch her back. "Come on back tomorrow."

As Arnold and Matthew jogged toward Jeb's house, Nancy asked, "How's that cut on B. K.'s leg?"

"It's healing up." Bertie picked up a slate and piece of chalk. With a sheepish grin, she sat down. "You got another minute, Miss Nancy?"

"Sure."

"Let me try to draw the letters you taught them today."

The moon must be full. It's almost as light as day. Nancy jumped from her bed. Gunshots sounded from the direction of Jeb's place. Goosebumps covered her arms, as a chill ran through her.

Although she seldom succumbed to fear, she couldn't contain her feelings.

Double-barreled shotgun ready in her hands, she crept to the front room window and sat. Grover's low menacing growl announced the presence of intruders. Sparks of light flashed followed by the crackling sound of fire.

She moved the curtain enough to see outside. Four men in white robes, which must have been constructed from sheets, and floppy pillow-case hats frolicked around a burning cross. *Ku Klux Klan don't want us hanging around with the Barneses.*

Amos had called them cowards. Otherwise, why would they hide their identity?

She took aim. *Got to protect Tommy and me.* A well-placed shot fired above their heads.

They scampered toward her gate. Had they tied their horses to her fence?

She crept to Tommy's room, where he lay still in his bed.

"It's okay, son." She pulled him to her in a hug. "They won't come back."

At least not tonight.

Chapter 10

Nancy sat by Tommy's bed.

"What about the fire?"

He must have taken a quick look out the window and scampered back under his cover.

"Come here."

He jumped into her arms.

She held him so he could see out his window. "The fire's in a clear place, and I'll watch it. I expect it will burn down and stop. Now go back to sleep. Everything's okay."

He lay down again.

She stayed in the chair beside his bed and rubbed her lower back as she watched him.

What will the Klan do next?

Amos kept a pistol in the drawer of his bedside table. Did he take it with him? She could handle the shotgun well, although it kicked her if she wasn't careful. It would help to have the pistol secured in a tight pocket of her skirt all the time.

She crept from Tommy's room back to her bedroom and found it with plenty of ammunition.

The earlier noise of gunshots in the direction of Jeb's place flashed into her mind. Were he and Evie all right?

Meanwhile Jeb sat inside his unfinished house in the light of the moon shining through a window. It was a mess in the midst of incomplete construction. At least it worked better than the wagon they'd called home.

A fire crackled in his front yard. *Oh, no. All the hard work. The money. None of that matters though if I don't protect my baby girl.*

Through a window he saw a cross burning. Four men in white robes and pillowcase hats danced around it. He grabbed his shotgun. "Don't move, Evie."

He fired a shot upward. The men started to scurry away. Jeb grabbed his pistol in his right hand and Evie in his left.

Make them dance! Before they could get away, Jeb sent bullets near their feet and watched them dodge.

"Hold on, Evie." Jeb grabbed his rifle. "We need to go outside. Could you sit in the wagon a minute?"

"Okay, Papa."

Quickly he loaded her into the wagon and poured buckets of water onto the burning cross, close to his lumber pile.

He took his daughter into his arms. "Come on, Evie. They're gone now."

Jeb jostled Evie in his arms until she slept. Then he went to sit by the front window. Despite the danger they faced, he dozed.

Bang-bang! Two shots rang out from the direction of Nancy's house. *Her double-barreled shotgun, no doubt. I need to check on her, but it's too dangerous to take Evie out there. Lord, please watch over Nancy and Tommy and us.*

On Sunday, Nancy tossed a dark blue cape over her shoulders. "Tommy, you'll need to wear your light jacket."

Jeb showed up wearing a gray suit with a white shirt. His marvelous physique, his deep-set blue-green eyes, and his auburn curls flying in the breeze made him look handsome enough to turn any woman's head.

Jeb pushed his hat in place. "Since I needed something a little warmer to wear today but not too warm, I decided to wear my suit. After all, it's church."

Nancy inhaled a deep breath and sighed. "I see. I'm glad Evie has that cute sweater to keep her warm."

Nancy dared not let him catch her looking his way.

They rode along in silence. Nancy prayed. *Lord, please bring Amos home soon. I need your help today. My neighbor has started to attract my attention in a way that doesn't honor my vows. I cannot look at a man as long as I'm married to Amos.*

Before the church service started, Deacon Harter stood. "I have an announcement. There's a cyclone blowing onto the Gulf Coast. It's done a lot of damage. We can expect rain. The storm is why we're having this cool snap."

On the way home after church, Nancy fluttered her eyes. "Would you and Evie care to eat a bite of lunch with us?"

Jeb toyed with the horses' reins. "What's on the menu?"

She grinned. "That's not polite."

"Well, what are you having?"

"Collards and peas I left warming on the stove, pickled beets, sliced onions, boiled eggs, and apple pie."

"Mrs. O'Reilly, I don't know how you come up with so many good things to eat. I was only teasing. We'll be glad to join you and Tommy for lunch."

Why not? If Amos came home, she'd set an extra plate for him. He might ask her why she was having another man eating with them, but first her husband would have some explaining to do.

Jeb ate so much that Nancy wondered how many decent meals he was able to prepare. After lunch, he motioned to Tommy. "Let's clean the kitchen." Tommy scraped the plates while Jeb swept the floor. As they did those jobs, Nancy heated water in a kettle and poured it into the dishpan. Jeb in a playful way pushed her aside. "Nancy, you can wipe the table. Then sit here and rest. You must get extra tired these days."

"Whatever you say." She wiped the table, then sat.

He washed the dishes. "Tommy, you dry. Evie, here's a pot for you to dry."

Jeb poured out the dirty dishwater. "Now let's take a ride." They went outside, and he helped Nancy climb into the surrey. "We need to check on the cotton."

When they reached the field, Evie shouted, "Oh, no. The pretty flowers are gone."

Jeb laughed. "They turned into little green balls called bolls. Soon they'll open up into fluffy white cotton."

Monday morning, the clouds hung low. Nancy shivered while she stirred the embers in the stove. *Any day now, we'll need to build a fire in the fireplace.*

Tommy scooted into the kitchen and warmed his hands in front of the stove.

After Jeb took Tommy to school, the Barnes boys had their lessons and went to work on Jeb's house. Nancy and Bertie with Evie and Cora Lee following them rooted around in the garden for whatever remained.

On the way back to the house, Bertie stopped at the pile of ashes. "What happened here?"

"Oh, not much." Nancy sighed. "Klan came for a visit and burned a cross."

"Listen here, Miss Nancy. I don't want to cause no trouble. If it's going to make folks threaten you and yours for us to come around, we'll stay away."

Nancy raised her hand in dismissal. "Don't worry about it. If we back down, they'll just get worse."

Monday afternoon, a light rain started. It fell softly at first and picked up hour by hour. The wind blew hard.

When Jeb brought Tommy home from school, Nancy handed them towels. "Come inside and warm up."

Jeb lifted Evie and held her away from him. "Papa's wet from the rain."

Tommy dried himself. "Mama, teacher said no school the rest of the week."

As Jeb started to leave, Nancy handed him a pot of stew and a plate of hot cornbread. "A little something for you two on this cool wet evening."

Jeb looked deep into Nancy's eyes as he took the gifts of food. "This was awfully kind of you."

B. K. drove his wagon up to Nancy's front porch. Bertie and Cora Lee went out to greet him. He shook the water off his face. "When the rain slacks, I'll help you milk."

Nancy brought him a towel. "It's going to rain like this for days."

He took the towel from Nancy's hand. "Are you sure you want me to dry off with this here white folks' towel?"

"Yes, I'm sure."

"Since it ain't going to stop raining, me and Bertie will milk the cows."

"I really appreciate this." Nancy took Cora Lee's hand. "Can you stay inside with me a few minutes?"

Chapter 11

The next morning, as Nancy stirred the fire in the stove, Tommy peered through the window. "When will the rain stop?"

She inched over and placed a hand on his shoulder. "As long as we stay inside, we can endure it."

"I want to go to school. I miss Clay and Becky."

"Your friends?"

"Yeah, Mama."

"I hate to see you miserable." She turned his face up to her and squeezed his cheeks. Then she went back to check her fire in the stove.

Tommy pointed outside as he pressed his nose against the windowpane. "Mr. Jeb and Evie coming."

Nancy rushed over to the door and swung it open.

Jeb gave Nancy a tender look as he brushed water off his clothes. "Morning, ma'am."

"Howdy." Nancy offered Jeb two towels.

Jeb dried Evie and then himself. "Just came over to help you manage your chores."

"Mighty kind of you." Nancy couldn't imagine how gloomy her life would be without her neighbors.

"Tommy, come with me to the corn crib. We'll bring a load of nubbins to the house so you can feed the chickens on the back porch."

She took Evie by the hand. "Let's go to the kitchen. You can help me knead some dough."

In a short time, Jeb and Tommy returned. Once they placed the corn inside the back door, Tommy shucked a few nubbins, which he spread on the porch floor for the chickens to peck. He didn't have to call them. Tommy stuck his head inside the back door. "Mama, our chickens can fly."

"Let's go look." She led Evie to the back window, where the bedraggled rooster and hens with their sagging feathers flew to the porch to peck corn.

The little biddies with their heads turned upward took water into their mouths. Jeb caught them in his quick strong hands and placed them in a crate. "These little fellows are about to drown." When the hens finished eating, they flew to the trees. "Too bad they left their babies."

Nancy found towels for Jeb and Tommy. "Come on inside. Me and Evie stirred up some molasses teacakes."

Nancy pulled the hot teacakes from the oven and served them.

"So good." Jeb bit into the snack. "We've got to keep milking or Flossie and Bella will dry up."

Nancy motioned with her hand. "One or two misses won't hurt."

"Mrs. O'Reilly, you are a fine cook." His small plate emptied, he reached for seconds. "I found some rope. If it's all right with you, I'll lead your cows to my barn. It is on a higher elevation."

She brought her hands to her mouth. "You'd do that for us? I'm touched."

He spread his arms. "We do whatever we need to."

As Jeb started out the door, Nancy took the little girl's hand. "Evie, stay here with Tommy and me."

A few minutes later, Jeb returned with water dripping from his clothes. As he stood on her front porch, he handed her fresh milk. "Now I'll move your mules over to my place."

She dried his face. "You're going to get sick."

"Thanks." He closed his eyes and opened them wide.

She winked at him. "What about the pigs?"

He chuckled. "Can't help the poor pigs except to throw them some hay."

As she stood on the porch, she shivered in the cool damp air. "It'll take a lot of hay."

"Yep. B. K. will bring his cow and mule over to my barn too." He reached his arm around her and opened the door. "Be careful. The floor's wet. I wouldn't want you to fall."

She held onto him to walk back inside. When she had sure footing, he left.

Such a wonderful friend. Amos would be glad Jeb is seeing after us.

The constant rainfall continued. Returning from Jeb's barn, B. K. and Bertie brought fresh milk in a sealed lard can to Nancy. Their three children followed them like wet ducklings.

Nancy took the can from B. K. "Much obliged."

He stared at the ground. "Miss Nancy, could we sleep in your hay crib?"

"Sure." Nancy set the milk on the little table on the porch. "I bet you can't even get near your cabin. You must have had to wade through water to get here."

"Yeah, we did. Cohay's done overflowed its banks. At our place it's three feet high. I've seen worser floods, but this one's awful enough. It ain't in our house, but it's miserable."

"Snakes." Cora Lee tugged on her mother's dress. "Scare me."

"I know. I'd be scared too." Nancy leaned down toward the little girl. "Don't you need to eat supper?"

B. K. slung rainwater from his face. "I don't know how I'm going to feed my family tonight."

Bertie stared into the distance.

"Tell you what." Nancy reached her hand toward them. "I've got plenty of food. Bertie, could you help me stir up something for us?"

Bertie spoke in a quiet, stern voice. "Yes'm, I'll help."

All the Barnes family but Bertie sat on the porch while the women went to the kitchen.

"Let's see, Bertie. I've got some leftover sweet potatoes. We can peel them and fry them in butter."

"You want them sliced thick?"

"Sure. Like you probably fix them." Nancy stirred batter for hoecakes.

In a few moments, the women served steaming plates of hoecakes with butter, molasses, sweet potatoes, and fresh milk.

Jeb arrived and grabbed a plate.

After B. K. cleaned his plate, he shook his head. "Mighty good of you, Miss Nancy. I don't know what we're going to do though. I thought we'd get ahead this year. We had the finest cotton crop I've ever seen. Now the green bolls have broke off the plants."

Bertie's voice had a bitter tone. "We've lost another crop."

"Water standing in the middles. I laid it by just like Mr. Amos showed me, but the flood's done got too high for that to matter."

"Some years have been good." Bertie seethed with anger. "No wonder the government deeded us this land. It was too close to the creek."

B. K. placed an arm around Bertie. "Don't give up, sunshine. We've finally found some land we can call our own."

Bertie pulled away. "After all these hard years of sharecropping and moving around from one farm to another. I know how you like to farm, and you're good at it. We can try to make it through one more winter. Then I say it's time to move to Chicago."

Nancy laid her plate in the stack. "I'd hate to see you go. If you really plan to leave, though, we've got work to do. You shouldn't go off without knowing how to read and write. Folks will take advantage of you if you can't read, sign your name, and make change. From now on, we're going to double up on the lessons."

The following morning the sun came out, and the rain stopped. Pools of water stood in the low places in front of the O'Reillys' house.

Nancy kneaded a giant pile of biscuit dough.

Jeb and Evie brought milk.

Nancy met them at the door. "Come have some breakfast."

"Wait a minute. Let me get some of this mud off my boots." He scraped the soles on the steps. "Would it be too much trouble to bring breakfast outside? We can eat on the porch."

"That will be just fine. Give me a minute. Tommy, come help carry the butter and molasses."

Nancy returned with plates and forks. Then she went back for coffee for her and Jeb and milk for the children. "Breakfast on the way."

She brought out fried ham, scrambled eggs, and biscuits on a platter.

"Miss Nancy, you make mighty fine biscuits."

Tommy and Evie nibbled, then played with Tommy's blocks.

Jeb reached for one more biscuit. "Until it dries up, I'll work on finishing the inside of my house. B. K. and his boys will come and help me when they can."

Nancy gave Jeb a look that showed she had something on her mind. "Don't you have some narrow pieces of wood that you aren't using?"

"Yes. Scraps. Why?"

"I want you to design curtain holders over your windows. In some of the rooms you might want valances. Other places you may want curtains."

"Oh, okay."

As Nancy and Jeb sipped their coffee after breakfast, the Barnes family, rumpled in their clothing and hay stuck in their hair, came stumbling across the front yard.

"Good morning," Nancy called. "Just in time for breakfast."

"You don't mind, Miss Nancy?" B. K. rubbed his belly. "We sure could use something to eat. That was a mighty fine supper you and Bertie cooked last night, but we done got hungry again and still no way to get to the house without wading."

The week moved along with the three families struggling against the water, which receded a few inches each day. Jeb told Nancy he'd return her livestock when the barn dried out.

Sunday came, but Jeb didn't try to drive to church.

Another week brought conditions closer to normalcy.

On a late September Sunday afternoon, Nancy rested on the porch.

Tommy leaned against her. "Whatcha making, Mama?"

"I'm tatting lace for our baby's bonnet."

"We're having a boy. I want a brother."

She tousled his hair. "I think the baby's a girl, but if we have a boy, I'll use this lace on something for Evie."

Felton Oglethorpe stopped his mule-pulled wagon in front of Nancy's porch. "Whoa!"

Nancy stayed seated, and Tommy sank into a nearby chair. She looked up from her tatting.

Mr. Oglethorpe tipped his dark gray derby hat. "Good evening, Miss Nancy."

She stitched the lace.

"How are you this fine day?"

Disgust came through her voice. "I'm okay."

"I've been missing you."

Nancy grunted.

"You remind me of my mother."

She busied herself with the lace.

"I brought you and the boy some hoop cheese and crackers." He climbed out of the wagon, ascended the steps, and placed his gift on the swing.

Grover sniffed it.

He pushed the dog's shoulder. "Git out of here."

Tommy whispered in his mother's ear. "Tell him to leave Grover alone."

"You don't have to talk gruff to him," she said, but Grover growled.

Felton kicked Grover's teeth.

"Come here, Grover." She grabbed the dog's collar. With difficulty, she pulled him away.

Felton backed toward his wagon. "Sorry no-good son of a gun."

Her face grew hot with rage as she scolded. "Stop it!"

While she held onto the dog, Felton climbed back into his wagon.

"Sit, Grover." She poked a finger in the dog's face. "That's enough."

Grover whined and sat near her.

"I brought you something because it's my duty to help you out now that you're a widow."

She turned away from the dog and stared at Felton. "I don't know that I'm a widow. Perhaps you know something I don't."

"Everybody knows."

"I don't, and I wish you'd watch your tongue in the presence of my boy." She fumed within although she spoke in measured words.

"Have you seen any Klan activity?"

Her eyebrows rose. "Why do you ask?"

"No reason. It's good the Klan is working to preserve our way of life."

"Thank you for stopping by, Mr. Oglethorpe." She stood and walked toward her door. "Come on, Tommy."

That night, Nancy dreamed Jeb kissed her on the front porch and Amos showed up from the darkness.

She awakened perspiring. *I cannot control my dreams.*

Chapter 12

All it took was a little time. The ground dried up, and the hard green bolls opened into fluffy white cotton.

Amos had plowed many a Saturday evening until dark to grow that crop. Too bad he couldn't see the snow-white field spread out in its glory.

Nancy fought back the tears as she rode with Jeb and the children around the edge.

The next day started before sunup. Jeb held a little tablet and a sharpened pencil. "I don't mean to take over the management."

"I'm glad you are."

"Just doing what needs to be done. I'll get everybody organized. Then come back and take Tommy to school."

"You tell them I'm cooking dinner today. Feeding folks on the back porch at twelve noon."

He pressed his broad-brimmed straw hat on his head. "Ain't you a sweet lady?"

She rolled her eyes. "Come on, Evie. You're staying with me."

"I sleepy." Evie rubbed her eyes with her fists.

Jeb met the Barneses at the top of the rolling hill, where the cotton patch began.

All the Barneses - Bertie, B. K., Arnold, Matthew, and little Cora Lee - waited. Jeb passed out gunnysacks. "When you get your sack full, bring it to me. I'll weigh it and record how much you've picked. Then we'll empty it into the cotton crib. I'm gonna keep it locked up the rest of the time."

B. K. raised his hand. "We needs to go home at dinner time, and we'll come right back."

"Miss Nancy's fixing dinner and feeding y'all at twelve noon."

A mumble of pleasure floated through the family.

"I have to leave in a little while, but I'll be back as soon as I can. If any of you get your sack full before I come back, get one of these extras I'm leaving over here by the gate."

Sad the Barneses' cotton got ruined in the flood, but at least they can make a little money picking Nancy's crop. Never have I seen people pick as fast as Bertie and B. K.

Jeb milked Nancy's cows and took Tommy to school. When he returned, Bertie and B. K. had full sacks to be weighed and emptied.

He loved the smell of the fresh cotton. It had a pure, natural quality, fresh and clean but with the smell of the earth.

Shouldn't think about such, but it reminds me of Nancy. Mary Ann was attractive when she was in the family way. I dare not feel anything about Nancy except friendship.

He paid the pickers at the end of the day. When the cotton crib could hold no more, Jeb said, "Tomorrow, I need B. K. to go with me to the gin. After we finish taking a bale to the gin, we'll get back to work."

Jeb rapped on Nancy's door while the sky was still gray.

She swung the door open. She must have just gotten out of bed. He'd never seen her hair in braids hanging down on her shoulders. She held her unbuttoned robe over her nightgown. "It's early. Please excuse me for not being ready."

"Gin day."

"Oh, that's right." She extended her arms toward his daughter. "Come here, Evie."

"Get Tommy ready. I'll take him with me to the cotton crib. We'll load up, and I'll drop him off at school on the way to the gin."

She yawned. "I can get Tommy from school. I doubt you'll make it back in time."

"You sure? You'll have to hitch up the mules to your wagon and take Evie with you."

"Yes, I can do it."

He left his team tied by her front porch as he jogged to the barn to let in the milk cows. He milked Flossie first. "Flossie, you won't tell a soul, will you?"

Flossie swished her tail at a horsefly.

"That demon monster is on the warpath early today. Must be hungry."

Flossie swished again but hit Jeb's head.

"Ouch. Let me tell you a secret, cow mother. I'm falling in love with a woman who isn't available. Her husband must be dead, unless he deserted her, and I don't believe he would. She claims she wants her husband back. We need to find him so we can understand why he deserted her and that cute little kid of theirs. If he's alive, I'm falling into sin."

Flossie chomped on the nubbins in her feed shelf while Jeb milked. "If that weren't enough, she's with child. You'd think I'd lose interest in her, but she looks soft and at risk to dangers. I just want to scoop her up and take her to my house so I can protect her and her little boy Tommy from all the evils they have to fight."

When he stepped out of the stall, a thin gold line on the horizon announced the day was moving fast. "Thanks for listening, Flossie. I've got to get going."

He moved on to milk Bella. After finishing the morning chores, he took the milk to Nancy's house.

Tommy waited on the front porch swing.

They met B. K. at the cotton crib. The men loaded the wagon while Tommy watched. Jeb locked the crib, now half full.

"Y'ain't worried about folks stealing this here cotton?" B. K. asked.

"I have to trust the Lord to take care of us. Over at my house I left Cleopatra in charge."

"You want me to sit in the back on top of the cotton?"

"No. You sit up here."

Jeb, who had his pistol strapped to a belt, laid his rifle in front of B. K.

"This rifle tells me you're expecting trouble."

Jeb didn't say anything. They dropped Tommy off at school. "Okay, little man. Wait here for your mother to come get you at the end of the day."

The men doubled back to the road toward the gin.

B. K. said, "It ain't as hot as it has been. This here's a good-looking road. I don't ever go very far from my house."

The sweet gum leaves had turned various shades of orange, yellow, and brown. Since they were falling off and the brush underneath was dying down, Jeb could see more of the sides of the road.

Not as many places for bad guys to hide. Here's the spot where those two simpletons killed the rattlesnake they claimed they were going to eat for lunch.

Four men in white sheets and floppy white hats stood in the middle of the road. One of them held a rope tied in a noose to hang someone. The other three pointed guns at Jeb and B. K.

"Step aside." Jeb slowed his team to avoid a collision.

One stepped toward Jeb's side of the wagon. "Carpetbagger done come down here and stole a widow woman's cotton. Guess you sweet-talked her."

Jeb ignored the jab. He was not in the mood to convince them that carpetbaggers didn't come from North Carolina. Neither did he want to respond to the remark about sweet-talking Nancy. There was one comment though that he couldn't let pass.

"Widow? You said widow woman. What do you know that the rest of us don't?"

The other three stormed toward him, but he shot in front of their feet.

B. K. picked up the rifle and shot above them.

They retreated into the woods different directions.

"You're a good shot, B. K."

"Get my practice killing squirrels and rabbits for supper."

"It wouldn't have done no good for them to take our cotton." Jeb drove on. "Nobody at the gin would have believed they grew and picked it, if they're the bunch of ne'er-do-wells I think they are."

"Didn't you think they were going to shoot us?"

Jeb shook his head and chuckled. "Not really."

B. K. held onto the rifle. "You trust the gin owner ain't in cahoots with them?"

"Sure. He runs the gin to make an honest living. Farmers all around trust him. He's got no cause to hang with that gang."

"Suppose I do trust some white folk, but most of the time me and Bertie have been disappointed. You ain't from around here."

"So you decided to give me a chance." Jeb grinned. "What about Miss Nancy? You trust her."

"Well, of course. She's a good woman."

They rode on.

After the cotton was compressed into a bale, the gin owner paid Jeb in cash. As they rode home, B. K. prayed in a deep melodious voice, "Precious Lord, don't let those mean mens try to take Miss Nancy's and Mr. Jeb's money. Send your angels to guard us as we travel down this lonesome road."

"Amen." Jeb flicked the horses' reins. "Keep the rifle handy, but don't shoot unless you have to."

"Right. 'Cause if this here colored boy shot one of them Klansman, they come a lynching me for sure."

"You trade at the mercantile?" Jeb had been paying B. K. and his sons by the week for helping build the new house. "I mean you've made a little money. Y'all have enough to eat?"

B. K. took his cap off and rubbed his hair. "Can't say as we do. We be needing a few supplies."

"And you get them at the mercantile, right?"

"Nope, we don't." B. K. shook his head. "Colored folks ain't allowed in there."

"Oh." Jeb propped his leg on the front of the wagon. "I hadn't thought about it. We can work around that though. You just tell me what you need from the store. I'll get it for you."

"Thanks, Mr. Jeb." B. K. slapped himself on his knee. "Figure out how much it costs and take it out of my pay."

Jeb raised his voice. "Sounds like we got a plan."

"Bertie needs some cooking supplies. Flour, baking soda, sugar, salt. We like sardines when we can get them. And we need coal oil for our lamp and a box of matches."

"I can remember all of that." Jeb pulled a pencil and a paper pad from his pocket. "In case I forget something, I'll write it down in this little book where I've been keeping up with how much cotton everybody picked."

"I'll ask Bertie if she needs anything else."

"Mighty fine." Jeb set his horses' gait at a steady trot. They passed by the place in the road where they had trouble earlier in the day, and they made it all the way home without any unpleasant encounters.

Jeb handed Nancy the money.

She pressed a dollar into Jeb's hand. "Pay B. K. for helping you today."

Jeb placed it in B. K.'s palm.

B. K. held the dollar up. "That's too much."

Nancy beamed. "No."

As Nancy kept the money in her hands, Jeb, B. K., Nancy, and Tommy looked in every direction.

"Tommy, go see what Evie is doing." Nancy nudged his shoulders. "Don't stand around while grownups discuss business."

"Yes, ma'am." Tommy kicked the dirt as he walked away.

"We'll talk about this tonight, young man." She stood between Jeb and B. K. "It's not safe for a child to know too much."

B. K. walked over to the wood pile and leaned against it to take off his shoe. "Don't know where to hide my money. Guess I'll stick it inside of here."

"Be careful, B. K." Jeb looked in all directions then lowered his voice. "Go home and hide it. Can you come back in the morning to help me load the second bale?"

"Yes, sir." B. K. zipped away with a spring in his step.

Nancy counted the money. "Take out the money you're paying the pickers."

He took the amount from her hands. "Now you have fifty dollars, Mrs. O'Reilly."

"Half of it belongs to you." She pressed a twenty-dollar Double Eagle gold piece and five one-dollar bills into his palm, closed his fist, and wrapped her fingers around it. He tried not to notice the tingle he felt when she touched his hand.

Her face grew red, and she took a few deep breaths.

Jeb spoke with concern. "Nancy, are you all right?"

"Yes, I'm fine."

"Did the baby kick?"

"It embarrasses me for you to mention such things."

"Here." He handed back his portion. "Keep this. I don't need it."

She shook her head slightly. "I was prepared for you to say that. The last time I went to the mercantile, I saw a wood cookstove from Atlanta Stove Works for twenty-five dollars. You can pick it up day after tomorrow."

He exhaled and shook his head. "You drive a hard bargain. I can't turn you down on that one."

Nancy clasped her chin in one hand as she held her portion of the money in the other. "Where will I hide my money?"

Chapter 13

Nancy showed her twenty-dollar gold piece to Tommy.

"Can I hold it in my hand?" Tommy's eyes widened.

"Sure, son."

"That's a lot of money." He turned it over. "Where you going to keep it?"

"I haven't decided yet. Anyway it's best you not know. Don't tell anybody about it."

He handed it back to her. "Not even my friends at school?"

"No, Tommy. Don't tell your friends at school. Don't tell the teacher."

"Why?"

"It's safer that way." She smoothed his hair. "Besides, you wouldn't want your friends to think you were bragging."

After she was sure Tommy was asleep that night, she sewed the gold piece into the hem of her cape and placed the five dollars in her reticule.

The next day went the same as the first except that Jeb said, "You can pay me five dollars, but that's all."

This time she had two gold twenty-dollar pieces, which she sewed into the hems of two dresses that were too tight. The other money she placed in her reticule.

The following day, Nancy, Jeb, and Evie went to the mercantile. Felton sidled up to Nancy and handed her an envelope. "You've got a letter."

"Thanks." She inspected the return address. "Oh, good. It's from my family."

Jeb gathered B. K.'s requested items and piled them on the counter. "Could you add up the costs of these and give me a total?"

"I'll be glad to."

When Felton finished, Nancy stepped close to the counter. "I need to buy a few items."

He gathered the items she requested, and she paid him.

Jeb motioned with his head toward the corner of the store. "I want to buy that wood stove."

Jeb paid for B. K.'s supplies and the stove. He loaded the items into the front of the wagon.

Evie clung to Nancy as she would have her mother.

Felton and Jeb pushed the stove to the front door.

"Whew!" Felton stood and rubbed his back. "Let me get some help. Otherwise, we'll never be able to pick it up."

He walked over to the dice game in the shade of a tree and said something. The tall man followed him.

After they strained to lift the stove into the back of the wagon, Jeb handed the man a quarter. "Thank you, sir."

The man jutted his chin out. "Name's Clarence."

"Thanks, Clarence." Jeb nodded.

Clarence sneered. "It's Mr. Clarence to you."

Nancy and Evie sat on the wagon seat. While Evie licked a candy stick, Nancy read the letter.

Your pa has health issues. His gout prevents him from walking or doing much work. Please forgive me for saying it, but his disposition makes it difficult for me to take care of him.

I miss your sweet face and temperament, Nancy. Every night I pray that I might see you again. It's a shame that Tommy is growing up without my opportunity to observe him.

Give my love to Amos, Granny Willietta

As Nancy folded the letter, Felton's menacing tone caused her to look up. *What's going on?*

"Say, McAllister. You sure did go through the supplies you bought last week in a hurry. What are you up to?"

Jeb's mouth flew open as he turned toward Felton. "What do you mean?"

"I mean you better not be buying for no ex-slave that lives in your neck of the woods."

Jeb's face turned red. "You're in business to sell goods, and I make it my business to buy what I want. Money's money."

"I'm warning you, McAllister." Felton looked up at Jeb, who towered over him.

Nancy looked away.

Jeb grabbed Felton's hand and shook it. "We'd best be going. Have a good day."

"But, but -" Felton leaned back and frowned. "Don't forget what I…"

"See you next week." Jeb climbed into the wagon.

Jeb, along with the Barneses, picked the rest of the cotton field. B. K. said, "Another trip to the gin."

This time, Jeb placed his rifle in front of B. K.'s side and strapped on his pistol again. "In case we run into the dimwits."

B. K. climbed onto the seat. "Can't be too careful."

Along the road, they didn't see any other wagons, and their enemies didn't show up. As they rode home, Jeb frowned. "I don't think they've give up. May be looking for another place to attack."

"Like Miss Nancy."

"That's what I'm thinking." Jeb pressed his lips tight.

B. K. nodded. "We gonna need to watch out for her."

When they finished the day's work, Jeb said, "Meet me at the top of the field in the morning with all your pickers if you want to keep working."

At Nancy's house, Jeb handed her a twenty-dollar gold piece and ten dollars. He kept five. "Here's your money. Price of cotton dropped."

"That's fine." She looked up at him and smiled. "If it weren't for you, the cotton would have stayed in the field."

"Oh, I don't know. You would have managed somehow." He couldn't help admiring her for all she was able to do. He tried to deny the feeling of tenderness growing inside.

"As soon as you finish whatever you need to do, come on back and eat supper with us."

He stood facing her. "That's too much trouble."

"Not at all. I need to be sure Evie gets a good hot meal. Leave her with me while you do your chores."

Make sure Evie gets a good hot meal. Is that all? If Amos walked up right now, he'd have nothing to find fault with.

He took care of the livestock and went home. *Maybe Evie would like for me to wash my face, comb my hair, and put on a clean shirt.* He found a little bottle of spicy shaving lotion to sweeten up his scent.

Evie might like a little guitar music. So would Tommy. He placed his guitar in his wagon and drove the short distance to Nancy's house. Evie would need to ride home.

Supper was vegetable soup and cornbread fritters. *If Amos didn't have any other reason, he could have married this woman for her cooking. She takes the simplest food and makes it so good it's hard to stop eating. Where is Amos?*

After supper and cleaning the kitchen, Jeb brought in his guitar from the wagon. Without making any comment, he tuned his instrument and began to play. Soon he was singing "Buffalo Gals."

Nancy, Tommy, and Evie joined in. "Buffalo Gals, won't you come out tonight and dance by the light of the moon?"

Jeb and B. K. met as the sun rose.

"What we do now?" B. K. looked over the field, a mixture of brown and white.

"Second picking."

"We tried to get it all the first time."

"Impossible." Jeb dipped his head in agreement. "On top of that more bolls have popped open."

"Gonna take us longer to fill our sacks. But one good thing. The weather ain't as hot as it was."

"I'll up your price two cents a pound."

"Mighty thoughtful of you, Mr. Jeb."

"I estimate we'll have two more bales to take to the gin." Jeb scratched behind his ear. "And I'll need your help this time."

If this were my field, I wouldn't waste the time with a second picking, but since it belonged to Amos, wherever he may be…God rest his soul.… Since it belonged to him, it belongs to Nancy. I'll do the best I can for her.

After Jeb took the rest of the cotton, he announced, "It's time for haying."

"Be sure in the middle of all this farm work you let me teach the Barneses. B. K. and Bertie have learned to sign their names."

He gave her a slight hug. "That's fine."

She told him, "This is the best crop year ever. Amos would have been pleased."

"I'm proud for him." Jeb bit his lip and looked away. "I suppose it's time to cut the sugar cane and make molasses."

Memories escaped her eyes and rolled down her cheeks.

The coolness of fall felt pleasant, especially in the evenings and early mornings. Nancy's garden yielded new fresh vegetables - tomatoes, onions, collard greens, and beets.

She invited Jeb to supper again on Friday night. After they feasted on fried green tomatoes, cottage cheese, and a variety of vegetables, Jeb helped clean the kitchen.

"You always clean the kitchen. Some woman, either your mother or your wife, taught you well."

"Not really. I clean because it's a necessity."

Nancy poured fresh molasses into her big black skillet. "I'm fixing to make taffy."

"You should have let me help you." Jeb rushed over to the stove.

She laughed. "Okay. You can stir."

"I meant you should have let me help you lift the skillet and the tin of molasses."

"Naah. I lift stuff this heavy all the time."

When the molasses heated to the soft-ball stage, Nancy threw in a pinch of soda.

Jeb jumped back away from the foaming liquid. "Swoosh!"

"Keep stirring, but don't let yourself get burned."

He stirred. "This is amazing."

"Use these potholders and lift it over to the trivet."

"Stay out of the way, children." He leaned forward and grasped the handle to move the skillet. "Now what?"

"Let it cool."

After it cooled to her liking, she shaped it into balls and reached for the butter. "Tommy, let me help you roll up your sleeves."

Tommy unbuttoned the cuffs.

She rolled them up and buttered his hands. "Hold them out from you."

Jeb rolled up his sleeves and held his hands out for Nancy to rub butter on them.

She didn't look up.

Then she handed him a ball of candy. "Pull and fold."

Tommy pulled hard, but the job was difficult. "Mama, I can't do this. You do it."

"Wipe your hands on the dish towel. Then wash and dry them."

After Tommy cleaned his hands, he went and sat by Evie. "I'll read you a story."

Nancy buttered her hands. They pulled and folded the candy until it was ready to be cut into pieces. She looked up to find his eyes penetrating hers. An enticing warmth rushed through her. *I shouldn't have cooked taffy.*

"Cut it with the knife like this." She cut two pieces and handed Jeb the knife to finish the job.

Then they went on to the next mound…and the next…and finally the last one. By the time they finished, she felt warm and cozy with Jeb. *Lord, forgive me. Where is Amos?*

Saturday morning, Nancy loaded the children into the wagon to go to the peanut patch. She included tins of biscuits and boiled eggs, along with jugs of water. Grover followed them.

Jeb came later with a mule pulling a light harrow. He loosened the dirt in the middles of the rows.

Then he pulled the peanut plants and stacked them. Nancy went to work picking the peanuts. The pungent smell of the fresh green nuts filled the air with the sweetness of living on a farm and growing their own food.

Tommy and Evie, dirty faced and holding hands, stood in front of Nancy. "We want some raw peanuts."

"Can't let you have more than you can hold in your hands. You'll get a stomachache."

They held out their hands.

"Evie, I'll shell yours for you." Nancy took Evie's peanuts back and shelled them.

When Jeb finished pulling the plants up, he helped her remove the peanuts and loaded full croker sacks into the wagon.

"Don't you need to take your mule and harrow back?" Nancy asked.

"Nope. I'm not leaving you and the kids here. We'll all go back together."

As the day turned to dusk, Jeb finished loading the peanuts. Eyes closed and faces smudged with dirt, Tommy and Evie lay on full sacks. Nancy, leaning over on the seat, rested her head on her hands.

Jeb hid the harrow behind a bush and tethered the mule to the back of the wagon. He climbed in and nudged Nancy. "Wake up."

She jerked into a sitting position. "I need to drive."

He pulled her close to him and tucked her head under his shoulder. "No, I'll drive us home."

Chapter 14

Jeb set his jaw firmly. On the way from North Carolina, his father-in-law had forced the wagon train to move at an intense speed. Mary Ann couldn't stay awake because fatigue knocked her down. The way she lost their baby and then died left agonizing memories. He should have stopped, but they needed to stay with the group as they passed through hostile territory.

Here he sat on the seat of another wagon where he made a similar mistake with another woman, one dear to him but in a different way from Mary Ann.

I didn't push Nancy to overwork, but I could have stopped her.

He had no way to determine how far along Nancy was in her pregnancy except through observations and comments she'd made. They never really talked about it, but according to his estimate, the baby was due in two or three months.

If the baby comes tonight, she'll lose it. I may even lose Nancy.

As he held the reins with his left hand, he placed his right arm around Nancy and stroked her.

Amos O'Reilly, how could you leave such a fine woman and good boy?

He drove up to her front porch.

Grover barked as Nancy struggled to climb out of the wagon.

"Stay put. I'll come around to help you."

Evie and Tommy didn't stir.

After he climbed out, he held onto her tight as she brought her legs over the side.

"Don't jump." He stood her on the ground, and she balanced herself by holding onto the side of the wagon.

"Let me help you up the steps." He guided her to a chair. "Stay there."

"I hope you didn't strain yourself. I'm pretty heavy these days." Her laugh came softly.

He went back for Evie. As he passed by her with his little girl in his arms, he almost tripped on Nancy's sprawled out feet.

With Evie leaning over one shoulder, he found a quilt on a shelf. Using one hand, he unfolded it to form a pallet in the vacant corner of the kitchen and laid his daughter on it. "Go back to sleep, sweetheart."

He yanked another quilt from Tommy's bed.

Tommy stood rubbing his eyes as he propped himself against the wagon.

"Come on, son. You can finish out your nap on a quilt in the kitchen."

Jeb squared his shoulders. *Me tired? No, I've got my second wind.*

"Come inside, Nance." He led her to the kitchen table, where she collapsed into a chair.

Nancy laid her head on the table, and he smoothed her hair out of her face.

Looking startled, she raised her head. "I'll cook supper."

Jeb pushed his palm toward her. "No, I'll find something and warm it up."

With a thump, her head returned to the table.

Lord, don't let her lose this baby.

He started a fire in the stove. While the cooking surface heated, he went over and rubbed her back.

"Here are some leftover biscuits." He sliced them and fried them in butter.

Evie sat up a moment, then stood. "I'm hungry."

He washed Evie's hands and face. "Tommy, go wash up. Then come eat a warm buttered biscuit."

The children sat and munched on the leftovers.

Nancy woke to say, "I'm so sorry."

She didn't need to apologize. I should be the one, but if I did, I'd...I can't go there.

"Nothing to be sorry about, kitten."

It was past bedtime, but Jeb had work to do. A snack would be a good reward for all the labor of the day. He put a pot of heavily salted water on the stove to boil and poured fresh green peanuts into the hot water.

A few minutes later they came to a rolling boil. The strong smell spread throughout the kitchen.

Nancy perked up. "I'd like a few of those peanuts."

Jeb and Nancy feasted on the fresh green boiled peanuts until they'd created a mountain of shells. Evie and Tommy ate a few peanuts too.

"I'm so tired. Jeb, could you help the children to bed?"

"Let me help you first." He lifted her to a standing position, led her to her room, and eased her onto her bed. It was difficult to remove her shoes and stockings from her puffy feet and ankles.

He pulled the cover around her shoulders. "Good night, sweet lady. After the kids finish eating, I'll help Tommy to bed and take Evie home. Grover can eat some leftover cornbread and buttermilk. Don't worry about the front door. I'll latch it and go out the back."

Nancy didn't respond.

Jeb tiptoed out of her room.

Morning light came through the window. Nancy's tight feet tingled as she climbed out of bed and grasped the headboard until the room stopped spinning.

Tommy knocked on her door and entered. "Mama, are you okay?"

With effort, she put pep into her voice. "I'm fine. How are you?"

Tommy lifted his tear-streaked face up to her. "You slept in your clothes."

She gently wiped his tears with her thumb. "I was tired."

"Your face is red."

"We stayed out in the sun yesterday."

More tears streamed down his cheeks. "Papa's gone."

Why did he bring up that subject? She cleared her throat. "We don't know when he's coming back."

Tommy slammed the door hard. "He ain't."

"Come here, son." She reached out and pulled him against her for a hug.

He sobbed. "Please don't leave me, Mama."

She laughed. "What made you say such a silly thing? I'm not going anywhere."

He heaved as fresh tears rolled down his face. "I thought you were going to die."

"No way." She handed him a face towel. "Let's go find something for breakfast."

He devoured a bowl of cornmeal mush, a serving of scrambled eggs, and a stack of hotcakes.

She nibbled at the cakes. "After yesterday, I'm not surprised you were hungry."

"Yep."

She touched his arm. "You know we almost never miss church, but I think it'd be good to stay home and rest."

"Yes, ma'am."

In came Jeb and Evie. He said, "Running late today. I hope the cows aren't too upset."

Nancy stayed seated. "Pour yourself some coffee. You and Evie are welcome to share our breakfast."

"We ate, but don't mind if we eat a little more." He cut a hotcake in small bites for Evie. "This is good coffee." He buttered two hotcakes and poured molasses on them for himself. "Your food always makes me hungry."

She smiled. *I'm sorry my face is puffy. It must be a worrisome sight.*

A few minutes later, he stood. "Got to head to the barn."

When he returned with the milk, he took it to the cellar and came to the kitchen where he washed his hands. "Tommy, come over to my place a little while, and I'll bring you back. Nancy, we'll let you get dressed, and I'll come cook dinner. Let's go, Evie."

Tommy left with Jeb and Evie. "When we come back, can we boil some goober peas?"

Nancy stacked the plates in the dishpan. "Sure thing."

That afternoon, Nancy sat on the front porch in a long flowing dress and propped her bare feet up. Since her head felt tight, she let her hair down. She was so tired that whatever Jeb, Tommy, and Evie were doing didn't concern her. Her eyes felt more comfortable closed, and time bent in an unrealistic pattern as she dozed.

Grover set forth his urgent bark with no signs of stopping.

"What is it, boy? A terrapin?"

When she looked up, Felton Oglethorpe sat in his wagon next to her front porch. Something about his gaze repulsed her. Maybe it was the way he licked his lips, or maybe it was that he stared at her too long.

"Nancy." He spoke her name in a soft voice. "You didn't' show up at the mercantile yesterday. I looked for you all day."

So? She raised her eyebrows. Since when was she required to go to the mercantile every Saturday?

"And this morning when you didn't show up at church, I was good and worried."

Grover dared Felton to step out of his wagon.

"Hush, Grover." Nancy couldn't make the dog hear her, or if he did, he ignored her command.

"Shut up, dog!" Felton yelled. "I brought you some supplies. These are a gift."

"You didn't need to do that."

With his teeth showing, Grover jumped toward the man and growled.

Felton moved to the middle of the seat, his legs pulled tight in front of him. "Tie up your dog so I can unload these groceries for you."

Nancy lowered her swollen feet to the floor.

Jeb stepped outside. "Grover, hush."

The dog stopped barking reluctantly.

Jeb commanded, "Now come here, Grover."

The dog went to Jeb.

With effort, Nancy spoke loud enough to be heard. "I think it would be better if you keep your supplies inside your wagon."

"McAllister, you're treading on a slippery slope. If you get caught cohabiting out of wedlock with this woman…"

Jeb rolled his eyes. "Oh bother."

"You're going to prison."

When Tommy went to bed that night, Nancy said prayers with him.

"Mama, what does 'cohabit' mean?"

"Living together."

"Mr. Jeb doesn't live with us."

"Right, son."

"If Mr. Jeb comes to our house, will we have to go to prison?"

She squeezed Tommy's hand. "No."

"I'm scared, Mama."

When she stood to leave his room, she couldn't walk. A strong pressure on her back followed by a squeezing sensation kept her frozen in her tracks.

Oh, God. I pray this is false labor.

Chapter 15

Nancy piled pillows at the head of her bed and sank into place. As soon as she grew drowsy, she awakened with a desire to go to the bathroom. She got out of bed and used her chamber pot.

Thirsty. Nancy drank half a glass of water, nestled in her feather mattress again, and rested on the pile of pillows.

No more contractions. She drifted off to sleep.

The next morning, she awakened to the smell of dripped coffee and fresh biscuits. She heard sizzling. *Mm. Bacon.* It smelled wonderful.

After her feet hit the floor, she slipped into her robe, which was getting tighter. With effort, she slid on her house shoes.

Tommy and Evie sat at the table, where Jeb served them breakfast.

"Sit down, ma'am." Jeb set a plate holding a biscuit and slice of bacon at her place.

"Wow!"

He poured a cup of coffee for Nancy. "I was explaining to Tommy that you need to rest a few days until you feel better."

"Thank you. I'm going to be all right, Tommy. I got a little too tired. That's all."

"He's afraid for me to be here because he thinks Felton Oglethorpe is going to have us all put in jail."

She bit her lip. "We talked a little about it last night."

"I explained to him there's nothing Oglethorpe can do to us. Besides, I'm not living here."

She patted Tommy's hand. "It's okay, son. Don't worry."

The time came for Jeb to take Tommy to school. "Nancy, I'll take Evie with us so you can rest."

Nancy went back to bed, where she had a good cry, and slept until noon, when she realized Jeb stood looking down at her.

"You all right?"

"I'm fine." She pushed loose strands of hair from her eyes. "I dreamed you were here. Then I woke up, and you really are."

"I'm here to take care of you." As she stood, he took her hands. "Easy. Let's go slow."

She laughed. "Please leave the room. I don't want to embarrass you."

A few minutes later, she found him at the stove and Evie playing in the corner on the quilt he'd placed there the day before. "Something smells good."

"Chicken soup." He ladled up two large bowls and a small one of the steaming food while Evie climbed into her propped-up seat.

"How can I help?"

"Just sit." He asked a blessing, and she sat waiting for her soup to cool.

She fought back hot tears. *When was the last time I felt the baby kick?*

"What's wrong, Nancy? You look as though a dark cloud came over you."

"Oh, nothing. This soup is tasty." She waved his words away and forced a smile.

"Don't push me aside like that."

"Okay! Could we talk about it later?"

He pointed his head toward Evie. "Sure. I'm sorry."

"Soup and cornbread. What a wonderful lunch." She eased a few bites into her mouth.

Why does everything make me cry?

After they ate and cleaned the kitchen, Jeb laid Evie on the quilt. "Time for a nap."

The little girl closed her eyes and breathed the breath of sleep.

Nancy went to sit on the porch, and Jeb followed.

Oh my, the baby kicked. By the time Jeb sat down beside her, she had broken into laughter.

"You were about to tell me what was wrong."

She rubbed her belly. "Now nothing is. Everything is wonderful."

"Mrs. O'Reilly, I'll never understand women."

Nancy lounged on the porch rocker as though she had nothing to do.

Jeb took Evie home after she finished her nap.

Late that afternoon, Bertie came to milk. "Lawsy me, Miss Nancy. You look all swollen up."

"I overdid Saturday, and now I have to pay for it."

"You ought to keep right on paying. Sit around like you're lazy."

"I will."

"Let me and Mr. Jeb see about you. We don't need for this baby to come too soon."

Nancy had one question. "Could you keep bringing your boys over for me to teach?"

Time dragged by for Nancy now that Jeb and Bertie didn't allow her to run her household. Life had its good moments though, like the evenings when Jeb brought his guitar over and sang with the children.

Over breakfast one morning, she told Jeb, "You make good coffee, and you can cook. I'm the one who's supposed to do the kitchen work though."

"And I'm the one who wants to help save your baby."

"I've been planning to harvest the pecans with Tommy's help after school and on Saturday morning."

He poured a second cup of coffee for himself. "What a crazy notion!"

"While you're holding the coffee pot, could you refill my cup?"

"Absolutely not. One cup is all you get, and that's more than you need. Your job is to rest. Coffee interferes."

"Yes, sir." She feigned a pouty expression.

"Let me make a suggestion. Get the Barneses to pick up the pecans on halves." He opened his hands as he talked. "You keep half, and she keeps halves of all she picks up. Good idea."

After breakfast, she watched him clean the kitchen. Then back on the front porch, she reached into the tightly sewn pocket of her dress to feel Amos's small pistol, which she made a practice of carrying with her. Who knew when they'd need protection?

Chapter 16

Nancy gasped for breath. Her hands and feet stayed swollen even though she rested the way Jeb and Bertie told her to. As she sat on the porch with her feet propped up, she awakened from a nap and mumbled, "I'm going to die. The baby won't survive."

The door squeaked as Jeb walked out of the house. "Evie's taking her nap."

She pointed to a chair. "We need to talk."

"What's on your mind?" He took her hand.

Nancy didn't push Jeb away. To have done so would only cause regrets. She gazed at the floor, then fluttered her eyes as she looked up at him. "I may die. I've seen it happen to other women."

His Adam's apple showed he was swallowing hard. Still holding her hand, he whispered, "What can I say?"

"Don't." She pursed her lips and exhaled as much air as she could. "Listen. If I don't pull through this, would you take Tommy and raise him as your son?"

His voice was soft and tender. "You know I would."

"And will you take this farm?"

"That may be a problem. We'll talk about it later." He stood and bent over to hug her. "You're getting upset."

She panted. "Yes."

"Let me say something else, dear friend." He sat back in the chair. "If I should not survive for whatever reason, I'd want you to take little Evie and raise her as your own."

Chapter 17

Nancy sat around with her feet propped up. Her skin felt tight, and her ankles looked huge. She tried to smile when Jeb came near her, but she wanted to cry.

"I'm going to get Peggy Harter." Jeb placed Evie in the wagon. "She may know what to do."

Peggy returned in the wagon with Jeb. "You've got dropsy. This is one time I'm glad we don't have a doctor in these parts. He'd insist on bleeding you. That ain't safe."

"What can I do?" Nancy's voice sounded weak.

Peggy dug into her reticule. "Wear tight stockings."

"I can't put them on."

"I'll help you." She turned to Jeb. "Let's help her get in bed, but we need to prop her head up with pillows. Then step out of the room, please."

With effort, Peggy applied the stockings. "Now, do you want to stay here?"

"No, I want to go back to the porch if that's okay."

Peggy stepped to the door. "Jeb, come on in here and help her get back up."

Exhausted, Nancy returned to her chair on the porch.

"Listen to me, Nancy. You're going to have to leave off salt."

"We have fresh peanuts."

"Uh huh." Peggy bobbed her head fast. "And you salted them."

"Yes."

"I brought you some parsley. You need to eat as much of this as you can."

Nancy nodded.

"I'll come back tomorrow and help you change the stockings."

As a few days passed with Peggy and Jeb's help, Nancy regained her strength and her condition improved. *I've experienced a miracle.* She returned to a routine similar to her old one but with an effort not to exert too much energy.

The baby kicked, and she rubbed her belly. "We're going to make it."

Saturday afternoon, she felt a craving for fried apples and onions. Jeb had picked some apples and left them in a bowl on the kitchen table.

"Tommy, would you please go to the garden and pull two or three onions?"

"Come on, Grover." Tommy took a bag and headed to the onion row, down the hill at the edge of the front yard.

The chore was taking Tommy too long. Grover barked the way he did when he'd found a land turtle or if somebody he disliked entered the yard.

She stepped onto the porch. Four men wearing makeshift robes constructed of sheets and pillowcases pulled down to their shoulders with holes cut out for their eyes appeared in the front yard.

One of them grabbed Tommy and with his left hand held the boy in front of him.

The Klansman's right hand held a gun pointing at Tommy's ear.

Nancy stood on the porch while Grover barked and ran from one man to another. She yelled, "Let go of my boy!"

"Give us your cotton money, or I'll shoot."

At that moment, Grover yanked the sheet off the tall guy.

"Clarence. I thought I recognized your voice." *Got to outthink these featherheads.*

Clarence engaged in a tug of war with Grover over the sheet.

Nancy remembered to talk loud enough to be heard. At the same time she kept her voice light. "Say, I thought you fellows were supposed to come around at night. You must not be real Klansmen."

"It's because of Bubba," one of them hollered. "He don't like the dark."

Another one said, "He's scared of it."

The man holding Tommy lowered the hand grasping the gun. "Am not. The trouble is it's hard to get around in the dark without tripping. Don't you remember how Clarence fell that night we burned the crosses?"

So the one holding my Tommy is named Bubba.

"That ain't what you told me," One of the hooded men jibed. "You's scared of bobcats."

The other unidentified man added, "And coyotes."

Nancy joined in. "Do y'all know about the Cohay panther? I heard her a few nights ago."

Bubba clutched Tommy's shirt. "Boy, where's your ma's money?"

"I don't know." Tommy pulled with his body and kicked. "Let me go," he yelled.

"Tommy don't know where the money is. Turn him loose."

One of the unnamed guys slapped Tommy's face.

"Don't hit my boy." Nancy eased her way down the steps and gave herself cover behind a shrub. She reached into her pocket for her pistol and fired at the feet of the man farthest from Tommy. The dirt kicked up in front of the rascal.

The men jumped around as if they didn't know where the shot came from. The one holding Tommy loosened his firm grasp, and the boy pulled away.

"Run, Tommy." She didn't say where. "Run like crazy."

Grover took off behind Tommy.

"Give us the money," Clarence yelled.

Nancy stepped out from behind the bush. "Go ahead and shoot me. Then you won't ever find the money. Nobody but me knows where it is. Tommy knows the names of two of you. And he'll tell. Shoot me and you'll be hanged."

They froze in place.

She caught her breath while she aimed her pistol in their direction.

"We'll find it."

"Drop your guns. I can outshoot every one of you, and I don't have nothing to lose."

They looked at each other. One by one, they dropped their guns.

"Is the money in your cookie jar? Between your mattresses? Hidden under the front doorsteps?"

Nancy giggled until she snorted. "Go ahead and look."

Clarence walked sideways.

"Don't sneak around behind me." She stepped backward. "What you want is the money, right? Don't try anything funny."

One of the other Klansmen started to slink away. "Guess we'd better be going."

"Oh really?" Nancy asked.

Quick as a whip, he grabbed a gun from the ground and aimed it at Nancy.

She shot the gun from his hand.

He tried to stop the bleeding by grasping with his other hand.

Jeb arrived behind them and fired into the air. "The rest of you, put your hands up. Don't move until I tell you to."

Nancy kept her pistol aimed at them while Jeb tied them with ropes and gagged them with strips torn from their own sheets.

Clarence jumped up and tried to sprint away, but Nancy shot his ankle.

As Jeb tied the outlaws, Tommy and Evie walked into the yard.

Nancy placed a finger over her mouth to tell the children not to talk, and she motioned them into the house. "Good job, kids." She hugged Tommy and Evie.

Nancy whirled around toward the men lying on the ground. First, she tore a sheet and tied it around the wrist of the man who had tried to shoot her. Then she tied a strip of sheet around Clarence's ankle. "Jeb, give me your knife."

He handed it to her.

Resisting the urge to move too fast and trip, Nancy walked inside her kitchen and dipped the knife into a pot of hot water on the stove.

Tommy and Evie sat trembling on the quilt in the corner.

Nancy grabbed a jar of corn whiskey Amos always kept on a shelf.

"Stay here, children. Everything's okay. I'll be back in a minute."

When she returned to the front yard, she went first to the man she had shot in the wrist. "This is going to burn, but I'm trying to help you."

Jeb bent over the man. "Give me the knife."

She loosened the lid and poured whiskey into the wounds on both sides of his wrist, then she held the jar to his lips. "Drink."

The bullet had gone through his wrist and lay stuck on the opposing side of his hand. Jeb cut out the metal as the man cursed.

Nancy wrapped the wrist tight with strips of a sheet.

Next, she checked on Clarence. "Let's make a tourniquet and elevate his foot. Jeb, would you find something to prop his leg on?"

Now what? Jeb needs somebody to help haul them in. He can't take them to the mercantile and expect any assistance from Felton Oglethorpe.

Jeb stood over the men on the ground. "Don't dare move."

When one of the two unnamed men wiggled, Jeb kicked the nearby dirt with his cowboy boot.

"Water," Clarence begged.

"Nancy, I don't want you lifting the water bucket. Come stand over them while I get them a drink."

She held her pistol, now reloaded, in her hand and lifted her long skirt to avoid tripping. "Don't try nothing."

Jeb gave them fresh water and handed the bucket and dipper to Nancy.

She poured out the water. "I'll wash these."

Jeb stood over the men until Bertie came to milk.

Bertie placed her hands on her hips. "Lawsy me. You done caught the Klan boys."

"Me and Miss Nancy and Tommy did."

"Well, I'll be. I hope Miss Nancy ain't been working too hard."

"No. She used her pistol instead of that heavy double-barrel shotgun that kicks her. Hurry! Go get B. K. Tell him I need his help."

"Be right back." Bertie turned and ran.

B. K. showed up a few minutes later. "Whatcha need?"

Jeb walked a few steps away from his captives and talked softly into B. K.'s ear. "Go to my house and hitch my horses to my wagon. Drive it on back over here. Make sure my rifle with ammo is in it."

"Sure 'nough."

Jeb cupped his hand over his mouth. "We're going to load this bunch of outlaws up in the wagon and take them to Mize. There's supposed to be two or three deputies in town. Saturday evening, they ought not to be too hard to find."

"Yes, sir, Mr. Jeb. 'Bout now they's dragging drunks to the calaboose."

"Right. We need to hurry."

B. K. sprinted toward Jeb's house.

"Nancy," Jeb called. "Come back down here. I need your help."

She returned, pistol in hand. "Whatcha need?"

He turned away from the men and talked softly. "Help me guard this bunch while me and B. K. load 'em up."

With a determined look in her eyes, she stood over them as she aimed her pistol, which she held with both hands.

Jeb and B. K. dragged the men into the wagon and tied them with rope. "Nancy, keep your gun aimed at them."

B. K. faced forward on the wagon seat, rifle in front. Jeb faced backwards, pistol in hand.

"You want me to drive?" B. K. asked.

"Yes."

"Wait a minute." Nancy was already on her way back to her house.

She came back carrying a kerosene lamp and her box of matches. "You may need these to help you on the way back."

A warmth flooded through Jeb's being. *I love this woman's thoughtfulness.*

The four men sat still with terror on their faces, and the team of horses traveled at a fast trot until the wagon rolled into town.

Jeb found the folks at Mize amusing. *The Saturday evening crowd will be amazed when they see me in my worn-out hat and my work clothes riding into town with B. K. in his tattered overalls and straw hat. We may have to pay a big price, but we've got to do this.*

B. K. spoke in a trembling voice. "Me being colored, I ain't supposed to be on the front street, 'specially on Saturday."

"What's anybody going to do about it?"

B. K. kept going until Jeb read a sign that said *Deputy Lawson Jones.* "This is it. Stop here."

A crowd of Mize townspeople and farmers who'd come to walk the streets on Saturday gathered around them.

Jeb and B. K. kept serious expressions on their faces as they unloaded their prisoners.

The deputy, a tall man with a stern face, stepped out of his office. "What brings you folks to Mize?"

Jeb stepped forward, while he kept his eyes on the four men. "Deputy, my name's Jeb McAllister. This here's my neighbor, B. K. Barnes."

The deputy didn't offer a hand to shake.

"These four men were dressed up in sheets and robes trying to bully a woman, Mrs. Nancy O'Reilly, whose husband is missing."

The deputy removed his tan felt cowboy hat, ran his fingers through his hair, and replaced it. "Yes, I've heard of that woman. Amos O'Reilly's wife. Amos has been missing for months."

Jeb bobbed his head. "As I was saying, they threatened her and her kid. Said they'd kill both of them if she didn't give them the money she made from her cotton crop. They claim they're members of the Ku Klux Klan."

"And you tied them up with their sheets?" Deputy Jones smirked.

"Mrs. O'Reilly shot two of them with her pistol. One in the wrist in self-defense and the other in his leg when he tried to run away."

"What a woman!" The deputy's eyes narrowed, and he looked over the men. "Let's get a closer look."

Jeb reinforced the bandages while the deputy checked the men out. By then, two other deputies appeared on the scene.

Deputy Jones motioned with his arm. "Let's get them into the calaboose."

B. K. stepped back into the wagon. This time, Jeb held the reins. They rode up the street through the parting crowd. As the sun set over Mize, they rode east.

When bedtime came, Nancy read to the children.

"Evie, I'm going to let you sleep with me in my feather bed. First, though, let's go with Tommy to say prayers."

After they read and prayed, Evie climbed in, and Nancy pulled the cover up around her. "I'll come to bed in a few minutes."

Nancy slipped out to the front porch, where she sat with Grover under the stars to wait for Jeb and B. K. to return. Dark clouds blew overhead covering the starlight, and thunder roiled in the distance. A powerful crack of lightning struck a tall tree in the front yard. Thunder shook the house. She crouched low as she went inside.

Chapter 18

As the night wore on, the storm blew past, and a hush fell over their house. Tommy lay still in his bed as his door squeaked. The house was so quiet he could hear his mother's ragged breaths.

When he'd been captured by that man called Bubba at pistol point, Tommy had been scared out of his mind. Now, he waited for Mama to come check on him, as she often did. She walked into his room. Tommy stayed still so she'd think he was relaxed.

The door squeaked again. He waited until he heard her drop into her bed before he sat up. Without a sound, he crept to his window, where he gazed into the darkness. The crickets chirped their gentle hum. After his scary day, he couldn't shake the fear inside. A sudden noise outside made his heart race.

A gush of wind, leftover from the storm, blew hard enough to cause the trees to sway. Only the noise of the wind. How silly to be frightened. His mom had always told him not to be afraid of the weather.

Back in bed, he drifted off to sleep, but when he turned over, he heard the distinct noise of horses and a wagon. He lay still and watched a light go by.

The world outside his window grew dark again, but he couldn't go back to sleep. A few minutes later he heard the horses and wagon return. The light passed from the opposite side of his window.

He lay staring into the darkness for a long time.

Strange that Grover didn't bark.

The rooster crowed and awakened him.

He must have fallen back to sleep.

The panther screamed in the distance.

Carrying his quilt and pillow, Tommy crept to his mother's room and fixed a pallet on the floor.

With the coming of dawn, Nancy awakened and stretched. Evie lay curled in a ball next to her. Tommy slept in the corner on his quilt.

Nancy pulled on her robe and went to Tommy's room to freshen up. In the dim light coming through the windows, she made her way to the wood stove in the kitchen. Since she had no matches, she hoped for embers left from Saturday night's fire.

Yes.

She placed a few small sticks of kindling on them and blew the glowing chunks to make the fire ignite. Once the kindling blazed, she added a few pieces of wood. A greased skillet warmed in the oven. While the oven heated, Nancy sifted flour and kneaded biscuits. With a potholder, she removed the skillet, which she filled with hand-formed biscuits.

Her other skillet waited on the stove. She dropped a glob of butter into it. As it heated until it sizzled, she cracked eggs, which she checked for freshness in a separate bowl one at a time, and added them to the butter. With a big serving fork, she scrambled them. Amos liked his eggs fried, but throughout her pregnancy the texture of raw yellow yolks on her plate had repulsed her.

With the breakfast ready, she brewed fresh coffee and poured milk for Evie and Tommy.

The children took their places at the table.

"Go wash your hands."

Tommy led Evie to the wash pan. "Come on. Let's wash up."

"And dry them." Nancy scraped the eggs from the frying pan with a spatula and placed them on a platter, along with the biscuits, some fresh butter, and a pitcher of new molasses.

As they bowed their heads, Evie templed her hands in front of her.

Tommy asked, "Mama, can I say grace?"

"Go ahead, son."

"Dear Lord, thank you for my mama and for this breakfast she has prepared. Thank you for not letting that man shoot me. And one more thing, was that light I saw in the night Mr. Jeb taking Mr. B. K. home? In Christ's name, Amen."

Nancy broke Evie's biscuit into bite-sized pieces.

Evie peered up at Nancy with a big smile. "Stir my molasses and butter together."

"Like this?"

Grasping her spoon in one hand and a piece of biscuit in the other, Evie smacked her lips and bobbled her head. "Yes, ma'am."

Tommy served himself a biscuit and some eggs. "I'm going to make a sandwich."

As the sun cast a golden glow through the windows, the children filled their mouths with delicious breakfast. As Nancy took one bite, Grover let out a friendly bark of recognition.

Jeb, in disheveled clothes and with a dirty face, stumbled into the kitchen.

"Papa." Evie, whose mouth was full of biscuit, scampered to him with excitement.

He lifted her high, kissed her cheek, and placed her back inside her elevated seat.

Tommy stared at Jeb as he sat down at the table.

"Good morning, Jeb." Nancy smiled. "You remind me of a horse that's been rode all night and put up wet."

"You could say that, Nancy."

"Hungry? We've got plenty."

He rubbed his bloodshot eyes and combed his hair with his fingers. "Excuse the way I smell."

It's the smell of a sweaty, hard-working man, but I like it.

Nancy handed him a plate and poured him a cup of steaming coffee. "Is B. K. all right?"

"Yes, he's fine. Nobody messed with him." Jeb served himself some eggs and piled three biscuits on his plate. "I took him home."

Tommy grinned.

"You took a big risk going into town with a colored man."

"Not much of a problem compared to what those men did." Jeb's voice shook with emotion. "All for a few gold coins those idiots tried to kill two people I love."

Nancy's eyes twinkled.

"You're a brave man, Jeb."

"I'm not half as brave as you and these kids."

After breakfast and milking, Jeb did the chores with Tommy's help, then put the milk in the cellar and returned to the kitchen. "We'll go on home, now, Mrs. O'Reilly. Much obliged for taking care of my little darling last night."

"My pleasure." Nancy dried the plates. "Don't think we'll make it to God's house this morning. He'll understand."

"Right." Jeb lifted Evie into his arms.

"Come on back in a little while to eat dinner. Don't sleep all day. You'll mess up your schedule."

Jeb and Evie went back home after the noon meal. Nancy and Tommy rested on the front porch, where Tommy took a nap.

As Nancy sat with her bare feet propped up, she gazed out at the garden on the edge of her yard. It wasn't a yard with green grass to be mowed. Instead, it was scattered with trees. Wildflowers in no particular pattern covered some of the ground. Other places were bare, hardpacked clay dirt. She couldn't imagine how some women…and men…could afford to fuss over formal gardens that yielded no fruit.

Despite the relief of having the Klansmen in jail, she still had a heavy heart. Hardly a day passed that she didn't wonder what happened to Amos. If he'd come home to her, she'd make it clear to Amos that any pleasant interaction with Jeb was merely friendship. Amos would have to understand that she and Jeb had depended on each other for survival.

As she sat lost in thought, she heard a wagon approaching. Jeb? No, it was Felton Oglethorpe. What now? How she despised that man.

He pulled up near her front steps. "I brung you a letter."

This afternoon, he didn't ask her why she didn't come to the mercantile on Saturday. Did he know? He didn't mention church.

Grover growled and made a fierce show of his teeth.

"I'm not going to step out of my wagon if you can't control your dog."

Her head pushed back, she stared at him.

"Well, do you want this letter or not?"

"You know I do."

"Looks like it's from your folks. Same address as the last letter you got a while back."

Nancy lowered her feet and stood. She trod, still barefooted, down the steps and around the wagon. "Grover, stop it. Hush."

Grover continued to bark.

She reached up for it.

"Not so fast." He held the letter out of her reach. "Nancy O'Reilly, you are a magnificent looking woman, even when you are with child."

"Stop it. Give me the letter." Anger made her chest heave.

"Okay." He sounded indifferent. "Let me put it in your hand."

"Hand me the letter."

He grasped her hand and kissed it with a noisy smack. "Here you go."

"You'd best be going, Felton."

After he left, she carefully opened the envelope and read.

Dearest Nancy,

Hope you're doing well. I miss you every day.

As soon as the weather cools but before it turns cold, I plan to load your pa into the wagon with as much other stuff as it will hold. One bright morning, we're going to head your way. Give my love to Amos and the boy.

I love you with all my heart. Granny

Chapter 19

"What's the trouble?" Nancy asked Bertie. "You've been crying."

"I'm so mixed up."

Nancy motioned toward a chair on the front porch. "Let's talk about it."

Bertie sat, and the two women watched a glorious sunset of pink, gold, and purple.

Nancy waited. "It's okay if you don't feel like talking."

"I has to talk. This can't be helt in."

"What is it?"

More giant tears streamed down Bertie's face. "My heart is so heavy."

"Take your time."

"My heart is heavy on the one hand, but it's light with joy."

"What's going on?" Nancy kept her voice mellow.

"B. K.'s brother."

"Is he all right?" Nancy asked.

"Yes, yes. B. K.'s brother and them coming through here in three days."

"How can I help you get ready for the visit?"

"That ain't it. We all moving to Chicago."

The baby kicked, and Nancy grabbed her belly. "You're going to move? I thought you were planning to move in the spring."

"It ain't safe for us here no more. After them four Klansmen get out of jail, they'll come for us. Maybe burn down our cabin. Or some more of 'em'll come after us."

"I understand." Nancy's voice quivered.

"B. K.'s brother, Isaiah, has made the travel arrangements."

"You'll need some money. Y'all come over here in the morning."

"Whatcha gonna do?"

"Buy your livestock." Nancy spoke with determination. "Jeb will be here to milk the cows. He can help me with this."

Bertie jumped from her chair. "Oh, Miss Nancy, I have to give you a hug."

"Yes." Nancy fought her tears. "I'll miss you so much."

"We's got to do what's best for our family."

"Tell me something, Bertie. How did y'all know about it?"

"Isaiah sent us a message through the grapevine."

All Her Dreams of Love

After Tommy went to sleep, Nancy ripped open the hem of one of her dresses. She was going to miss teaching the Barneses to read and write. She and Jeb would be hard pressed to find someone else to work for them at any price. B. K. wouldn't be around for the hog killing. Bertie had planned to be Nancy's midwife. B. K. had risked his life to help Jeb. All those reasons were nothing compared to the genuine love she had in her heart for each member of the Barnes family.

The following morning, Nancy, Jeb, B. K., and Bertie met on Nancy's front porch while Evie and Cora Lee played with Tommy's blocks.

Nancy looked up at Jeb. "I want to purchase the Barneses' milk cow, two mules, and whatever chickens we can catch. I'll also buy the hay and corn they have in their cribs."

Jeb frowned. "What's going on?"

B. K. shifted from one foot to the other. "We's moving to Chicago in two days."

"No!" Jeb swallowed hard. After a gloomy silence, he walked over and patted B. K.'s shoulder. "Since you have the opportunity, you better take it."

Because Nancy had proposed the sale, she spoke next. "Jeb, could you store the animals at your farm?"

"Sure. B. K., can you help me do that this morning?"

Nancy supposed she should have waited until after the delivery of the livestock to pay, but she wanted to pay the Barneses no matter what. "I'm going to hand the money to Bertie so she can keep up with it for you."

"Good idea." B. K. bit his lip. "Folks ain't as likely to suspect she has it."

Nancy handed Bertie a twenty-dollar gold piece.

"Whatcha planning to do with your plows and wagon, B. K.?" Jeb asked. "And harnesses?"

"Go off and leave 'em." B. K. looked away. "Don't need stuff like that in the city. Can't take it on the train."

"Would you sell that stuff to me?"

"Of course, Mr. Jeb. You can have all of that you want and give me what you think it's worth." B. K. turned to face Nancy. "Y'all feel free to pick our garden up there on top of the mound. We've got a fall crop of collards and turnips coming on."

In the middle of the morning, a parade consisting of two sway-backed mules pulling a broken-down wagon loaded with chickens in a crate and a middle-buster plow passed by Nancy's porch. A cow tied to the back of the wagon brought up the rear.

Jeb stood in the wagon. "I'll have to go back and get some more chickens as soon as I empty these out of the crate."

"When you come back by, would you take my trunk down to the Barneses?"

"Sure."

"I don't ever use it. They need something to pack their clothes in. Besides, my back room needs to be cleaned out."

Nancy would need a room for the baby eventually. Besides, Granny and her pa would show up when she least expected them.

Chapter 20

In the cool morning of the next day, Nancy perched in her favorite chair on the porch, a blanket wrapped around her and her feet propped up. Evie played with Tommy's blocks, and Grover lay curled in a sunny spot.

"You know, pup, this is hard." She rubbed her face. "We're going to miss the Barnes family."

Arnold and Matthew walked into the yard and up her steps. "We brung you something."

"Thank you." How she would miss teaching them and watching their young minds develop. "Hold on a minute. I have something for you. Stay right here."

They sat on the porch in the chairs where they had done their lessons. "Yes'm."

Nancy waddled inside and dug into her reticule for two one-dollar bills, which she dropped into her dress pocket. Back on the porch, she sat across from them. "You go first."

They handed her letters without envelopes. "We wrote these ourselves."

She unfolded one. "Dear Miss Nancy, thank you for teaching me to read and write. Matthew." And the other with the same message signed "Arnold."

"I'll treasure these always. When you move to Chicago, you'll get to go to school. Won't that be grand?"

They smiled and nodded.

"On the train, take your books and study your lessons." She pulled the dollars out of her pocket and handed one to each child. "Here you go."

"Much obliged."

She handed them a bag containing one of Amos's Sunday shirts and one of her good dresses, both dark, inconspicuous gray. "Take this to your ma and pa."

"Thank you, Miss Nancy."

As they walked away, she had no hopes she'd ever see them again.

While Evie took her nap, Nancy opened the door to the spare room and scanned the high piles of clutter. *Me and Amos have had a habit of keeping everything. Now, it's left to me to throw stuff away.*

It hurt to tackle the project. She knew from the first instant she stepped into the room she would encounter things that Amos had treasured. She'd throw away part of Amos.

I can't put this off another day. I must attack the mess.

Mouse droppings emitted a vile stench. *We need a cat.* The reason she had postponed the project became apparent. Until recently, stifling odors had nauseated her. Now, she could handle the smells. Also, she was glad the oppressive summer heat had passed.

Worn out trousers, shirts, and overalls had to go. She stuffed the old clothes into croker sacks and dragged them to the back porch. Couldn't overfill the bags. Shouldn't carry heavy loads. Frayed straw hats reminded her of the smell of Amos's sweat. They had to go.

Old dresses now in shreds, her hats out of style and musty, found their way into burlap bags. She dropped books yellowed with age and eaten by mice into worn-out wooden boxes.

Her back hurt, but she wanted to keep working. She shoved the sacks and boxes against a wall. Memories of Amos filled the room like the clouds of dust she stirred. Why had she left her diary, full of rose petals and letters from Amos, in the heap? She took it to the kitchen.

Need a breather. I'll check on Evie. A damp dish towel came in handy to wipe the book off. She set it aside by an open window to air out.

I should call it a day. Evie stirred from her nap, and pain shot through Nancy's back. She took the child to the front porch.

I hate to ask Jeb, but I need him to help me get rid of this mess.

All Her Dreams of Love

The clock chimed three...then half past. And four. Where were Jeb and Tommy? Nancy had had more practice waiting for the men in her life than she cared to think about. She wanted Tommy to come on home.

At the sound of the wagon, Grover stood and stretched. Evie yelled, "Papa! Tommy!" Nancy exhaled a heavy sigh. Why had Jeb worried her this way?

"Mama, Mama." Tommy started talking before he climbed down from the wagon. "Guess what."

She shook her head. "No idea."

"Miss Veronica fell."

"Really?"

"Yes, and she sprung her ankle."

"Sprained her ankle?" Nancy was relieved to have her little son home. "I'm sorry."

"Yes, and that ain't all. She couldn't stand up. Mr. Jeb helped her, but she was hurting so bad he had to pick her up and carry her."

Nancy could see that scene.

"He put her in the wagon and took her home."

"Oh?" Nancy felt her eyebrows going up.

"Tomorrow we're going to give her a ride to school in the wagon."

"She won't be able to walk. That's for sure." *Poor Veronica.* Nancy looked askance.

"That ain't all. Mr. Jeb is going to stay at school part of the day to help her."

Nancy turned her focus from Tommy to Jeb, who was staring at the ground. "How did it happen?"

"I'm not sure." He stepped out of the wagon. "She must have slipped on a patch of grass or a rock."

Evie ran into her papa's arms, and he lifted her. "Nancy, how have you been today?"

"Busy."

"Is Bertie coming to milk?" Jeb asked.

"No."

"If it's all the same to you, I'll go ahead and do it now."

Why was there a note of unpleasantness in his voice? Why would he not look at her?

Monday night when the moon was new, a blanket of clouds covered the stars, and the wind whistled relentlessly. Coyotes howled their musical sounds in the distance. The color of the night, the darkest shade of gray, almost black, hung so thick that the shadows of tree branches disappeared. Tommy awakened as twelve chimes from the grandfather clock announced midnight. Why did the clock disturb his sleep *that* night? Without making a sound, he crept out of his bed and stood by his window. The snap of a twig told him the Barneses passed by.

Two Sundays passed, and November brought a fresh chill to the air. Deacon Harter announced the plans for a Thanksgiving celebration.

After church Peggy Harter asked Nancy when the baby was due.

"Oh, I'm not exactly sure. Six weeks, maybe four. Late November, I think. Who knows? Maybe early December."

Peggy lowered her chin. "And you still don't have a midwife?"

"I had one, but she moved away."

"I'll write Cousin Iris and see if she can come for Thanksgiving. Maybe she can stay a few weeks with us and be close to you."

Since Jeb had taken the children for a walk in the woods, Nancy was alone. Had she not made it clear to Felton that she had no interest in him? Why did he drive his team to her house so many Sunday afternoons?

When she saw him coming, she didn't move. If she went inside, he might follow her into her house. That is if he felt brave enough to invade Grover's territory.

Might as well stay put and hear him out.

"You by yourself?"

She didn't hide her irritation. "What kind of question is that?"

"Men like sassy women. I like your feisty nature."

"You bring out that side of me." She wished he'd go away.

"Whenever we're around each other, sparks fly." He pulled off his hat and patted his hair. "Can't you see? We've got something between us like the charge of lightning."

"Stop it."

"Right now, you're as big as a cow, but it won't take you long to get your body back in shape."

She reached into her pocket for her pistol. If he made an inappropriate move toward her, she'd shoot. "That's enough."

He flashed his eyes. "Amos isn't coming back."

"How do you know?" She wondered whether he had some dark sinister knowledge about her husband.

"He's had all these months. It's obvious he's dead."

"Don't say that."

He stood and started to climb out of his wagon. "Me and you could have a good life together."

Grover, did you go on the walk?

At that moment, her faithful dog approached.

Felton sat down on his wagon bench. "Guess I'd better be going. Think about what I said."

Nancy stayed seated as he drove his mules away. No doubt Felton Oglethorpe was insane. He'd made it clear he wanted her, but why? Did he want a wife but was unable to attract one? Did he want her farm? Or worst of all, did he obsess over her enough to take drastic action?

Chapter 21

The wind blew so hard for three days that it rearranged the dirt, as it ushered in a cold snap.

Nancy reminded Tommy to wear his coat to church. Jeb helped her into the surrey, and she wrapped a blanket around the children's legs.

"It's hog killing time, y'all." Jeb's eyes met hers.

"Yes, it is."

"Well?" Jeb asked.

"What are my plans?" She gestured toward her belly. "We've got some fine hogs. If Amos were here, he'd plan to slaughter one right soon and invite the neighbors to come over."

"And if the Barneses hadn't moved away, they would have helped out."

Nancy pulled her blanket over her knees. "You do see that I can't do much about this, don't you?"

"Right." He clucked to the horses as they slowed.

"Let's set a date, say this coming Friday for the hog killing. and invite the neighbors. The Harters might want to bring one of their hogs over too."

"How do I do it?"

Nancy looked serious. "Don't make a big announcement. Most Sundays we have forty people in church. That would be too much. I do love a party, but we don't need too many workers."

"We've had a pretty large crowd at your house before. This time I don't want you to overdo."

"We need to invite no more than four or five families to help butcher. Let's see. The Harters and the Bynums. Who else?"

Jeb counted on his fingers. "The Smiths, Browns, and McCleskeys. We'll see which ones of them can come help."

"Sounds good," she said. "Friday we'll butcher the hogs. We can cook the meat overnight, and on Saturday we'll invite everybody to come to dinner. You'll have the next few days to find the tools you need and clean them up."

"I have to dig a fire pit so we can roast pork for supper."

"That will be wonderful. You're going to be busy this week." Nancy didn't know how much Jeb knew about the massive project of slaughtering hogs. *What if Amos should show up?*

Jeb stood outside before church and invited the men to come and bring their families. Harold Harter placed an arm on Jeb's shoulder to pull him aside. "Jeb, have you ever done this before?"

"I've helped with a few hog killings and done my share of butchering, but I ain't never cooked pork in a pit before."

"You're going to need some help with getting the pit ready and making sure the O'Reillys' smokehouse is in good repair. I heard you invite Steve Bynum."

"Right." Jeb nodded.

"I'll ask him if he can come with me, and we'll come over to help you get ready."

"Would Tuesday be a good day for that?"

"Yes. Steve has a contraption to roast pork in a pit. It's a set of old bed springs to lay the meat on and a metal barrel cut into halves. We'll see if he can bring it."

When the rooster crowed, Jeb couldn't go back to sleep. *Might as well get up early to have an opportunity to work on the house. Living in a place that's not sealed in ain't my style, but I've got too much to do.* He dressed, then tiptoed outside, where he built a fire in his outdoor firepit to keep warm and give him enough light to work. He checked his watch and placed it in his pocket. *Four o'clock.* Jeb measured and sawed pieces to be hammered in place later. Evie needed her rest.

The time flew by. He talked to the Lord as he worked. As he had done before they built the house, he cooked a breakfast of coffee, bacon, eggs, and hoecakes over the fire. Evie stumbled onto the porch.

"Good morning, princess. The smell of breakfast cooking must have woken you up."

"Morning, Papa."

After they ate and he did his barnyard chores, he hitched up the wagon to go drop off Evie and take Tommy to school.

The helpers showed up in front of Nancy's house on time as promised. When Jeb returned, Harold and Steve were drinking coffee as they warmed themselves by a fire in Nancy's yard. They dug a rectangular pit slightly larger than Steve's springs and barrel halves.

Jeb measured with his shovel on one end and the other to make sure the hole was an even shape. "This is as big as a grave."

Steve laid his shovel down. "I brung some rocks to line it with. We'll unload them from my wagon."

Jeb pulled a handkerchief from his overalls pocket and wiped his brow. "Y'all are mighty kind to help with this."

Harold placed Nancy's wheelbarrow near the back of the wagon. "Everybody thought a lot of Amos, and we're glad to help his widow out."

"Widow. Who says widow?" Jeb loaded rocks, each about the size of four bricks, into the wheelbarrow.

"Well, I don't know that Amos is dead," Harold said, "but it's starting to look that way."

They lined the pit with rocks until Steve declared that part of the job finished. "Next comes the wood."

Into the pit, they first dropped a thick layer of small sticks and brush for kindling. Then they loaded a few uncut limbs on the bottom and finished off with wood from Nancy's pile.

Jeb pointed at the empty wood rack. "Looks like she's going to need some more wood cut up before winter."

Steve gave Jeb a knowing look. "You sure are a considerate neighbor."

Harold pushed the wheelbarrow toward the storage shed behind the house. "As soon as I get back, we'll check out the smokehouse, and after that we need to fasten the chains to the tree limbs."

When Harold returned, he looked over the bedsprings. "We'll have plenty of room on here for the pig. It's going to take a lot of meat to feed whoever shows up Saturday. I'll throw in some roasts."

"Much obliged, Harold," Jeb said. "Nancy's already told me we could use whichever hogs we want. I think we need to roast a pig too."

Steve looked up at the oak limbs extending over the work area. "That means we'll need three chains."

After a morning of hard work and a tasty stew cooked by Nancy, the men finished their jobs.

"Everything's ready." Harold walked around to inspect as Jeb and Steve followed him. "The only thing left to concern us is the weather. If it stays cool like it has been today, we'll be in good shape."

"I didn't notice it was cool." Steve wiped his brow.

Friday, the five invited families rolled into Nancy's front yard hours before sunrise. They unhitched their mules. Some of the guests placed them in Nancy's paddock. Others walked their mules to Jeb's place and turned them loose in his little pasture.

Early Friday morning, Nancy stood by the fire the men had built in the pit. It took away the chill as it burned down in preparation of cooking the meat. She hugged herself and pulled her shawl tighter around her as she breathed in the smell of wood smoke in the crisp air. "We have plenty of coffee and sweets in the kitchen. You're all welcome to come have some."

"We will, Miss Nancy." Harold Harter tipped his hat to her while the men chatted about their week and warmed their hands.

"Everybody is in a good mood." She shivered. "I'll feel better after we get past the killing part."

Jeb smoothed her shawl around her shoulders. "Promise me you won't work too hard today. Just watch the other women and enjoy their company. Don't let yourself get too chilled."

She gave him a sweet smile. "I promise."

"Now go on back inside, where you can get warm."

She rushed back to the kitchen because she didn't want to hear the men strike the hog on the head with a hammer. The Harters' hog had already succumbed to a blow and waited in their wagon. And she didn't like to think about slaughtering a pig.

Three strong chains hung from sturdy limbs of oak trees. She didn't care to stick around and watch the men hoist the hogs.

Jenny Mae took Nancy's hand. "Come on inside, dear. Look at the couch."

A profusion of baby clothes, handmade by the guests, lay spread over it. Nancy threw her hands to her chin. "Oh, they're so…I don't know what to say… I love them."

The women stood around beaming while she admired each gift.

Tommy's teacher, Veronica Wilson, who lived with the Bynum family, turned school out and came for the day. She stood watching out the window. "Nancy, you ought to come look. Jeb cut their throats. Come see."

"That's something." Watching the animals bleed didn't interest her. She'd learned from her granny how to make *boudin noir* back at Port Gibson, but no one else around Cohay knew how. Besides, in her condition, she didn't feel like preparing blood sausage. Nancy, who had the responsibility to make sure certain jobs were done, pulled pans off the shelves and set them on the worktable.

"Look. What are they doing now?" Veronica pulled Nancy's sleeve.

"They're scalding them in boiling water. They have to remove the hair. It's easier to do if the skin is soft. Where are Tommy and Evie?"

Peggy Harter reassured her that they were playing with the other children. "Everything's fine. I'll make sure they stay inside."

It's odd that the children aren't hanging around with Veronica.

"Scraping time." Jenny Mae Bynum, who was tall enough to see over Veronica's head, watched the process. "If they didn't already have too much help, I wouldn't mind that job."

"Every hair has to be removed." Nancy remembered how Amos kept his big knife ready. Last Monday, she'd presented it to Jeb so he could sharpen it. As the men worked, she missed Amos.

Nancy joined the onlookers at the window. After the scraping, Jeb ripped open a carcass. Then he slashed open the other hog.

The men worked to sort the internal organs. While Peggy Harter watched the children inside and Nancy stayed with Peggy, the other women took pans out to receive the organs.

Veronica hurried over to stand in front of Jeb. That day she'd worn her long dark brown hair loose with a red ribbon tied to one small braid on the side. Her face turned up toward him, she held her pan so he could place sweetmeats in it. As she waited, she bounced and giggled.

The little flirt looking up at him with her big brown eyes. Her sprained ankle must have recovered. But what claim do I have on Jeb McAllister?

Veronica returned to the house. "I've never participated in a hog killing before. I'm from the city."

Pots boiled on the stove.

"Come here, Veronica." Jenny Mae stood on the side of the porch where she dipped water from the rain barrel. "I have an important job for you."

"What is it?"

"Everybody will be impressed if you do it well. Let me get you started. Roll up your sleeves." She put Veronica to work squishing the contents from the casings to be used for sausages.

Nancy stayed out of the row. *This looks like retribution for something.*

The men crossed the back porch and marched into the kitchen. Steve Bynum announced, "We've washed the carcasses. Now we're ready to take a break while they dry."

Jenny Mae huffed at him. "We're busy. You fellows will have to find your own noon meal. Get whatever you want from the table but leave us girls and the children something."

"Ain't you sweet?" Steve swatted Jenny Mae's back side.

Veronica threw the casings she was holding into the pan and washed her hands with lye soap. "I'll help you men find the food. I'm tired of this nasty job anyway."

"Pew." Steve held his nose as she passed.

She smiled at Jeb, but he frowned back at her. "No, that's all right. We'll find our own food. You need to go wash your hands again."

After the men ate, they cut chunks of meat. The women rubbed a concoction of salt, sugar, and home-grown herbs on the pork to be slowly cooked in the pit.

Endless jobs filled the afternoon, which had warmed enough to allow pleasant working conditions outside. When Jeb came to the porch and finished washing the casings, Veronica returned to help with the job.

She asked, "Will you use the same knife you used this morning?"

"No, I have a smaller one."

Veronica glowed as she spoke to him. "You were so masterful with the knife, and it was very sharp."

Jeb poured fresh water into a pan.

"I'm a very good cook. Maybe one Saturday I could come over and fix a meal for you and Evie."

All along, Nancy had been listening and watching. She stuck her head out the back window.

Jeb turned around and faced Nancy. "It's Amos's knife. Nancy let me use it."

"I've never helped with a hog killing before." Veronica raised her voice to a childlike squeal. "It's all so fascinating."

Jeb called out to Zack Smith, who stirred the contents of two washpots. "How's the lard rendering?"

"Good. We'll have some cracklings to share with the children soon."

Veronica brought a dishpan and stepped fast to keep up with Jeb as he carried a heavier pan. She pulled her skirt up with one hand and leaned the dishpan on her side with the other hand. "It's hard to keep up with you. You're so tall."

Nancy, carrying a mixture of seasonings in a bowl, trudged along behind them.

Pans of meat cut in pieces waited on the picnic table, where the sausage grinder was attached to the side of the table. Veronica stationed herself in front of Jeb and leaned toward him to inspect.

He dropped a piece of meat into the grinder.

Veronica, childlike, grabbed the handle. "I want to turn it."

Tommy stepped from behind his mother. "When teacher gets tired, it will be my turn."

Other children lined up behind Tommy.

Jeb backed away. "Y'all can handle this better than I can. I need to hang the hams and bacon in the smokehouse."

Veronica stopped grinding. "Could I help? I've never been inside a smokehouse." She touched his hand and stroked his arm.

Jeb grimaced. "Why don't you help Nancy with making the souse?"

Veronica placed her hands on her hips. "Souse?"

"Hog's head cheese." He strode away and called over his shoulder. "She doesn't need to get too tired."

A large pot of pig's feet, a pig's head, garlic, onions, carrots, vinegar, salt, and black pepper in water cooled on the stove. Nancy reached for her tongs. "This has cooled enough for us to work with."

Veronica stood close by, her lip curled and her arms folded in front of her. "How revolting!"

Nancy lifted the head onto a giant cutting board. "We need to remove the meat. Have you washed your hands?"

"I don't remember." Veronica went toward the wash pan.

"Throw the water outside and refill the pan, Clean your hands thoroughly. Scrub your fingernails. We don't want to make anybody sick."

Veronica, not saying a word, did as Nancy told her, then returned. "How about you? Did you wash your hands?"

"Yes."

Veronica grabbed chunks of meat and threw them into the big bowl. "It's a lot of work."

Nancy emptied the contents of the bowl back onto the cutting board. "Be sure you don't put any bones in the mix."

"You treat me like I don't have good sense."

When they finished preparing the meat, Nancy held the sieve and instructed Veronica to pour the liquid to be strained. Next, Nancy added more vinegar and salt and poured the liquid over the meat.

Checking it a final time, Nancy poured the mixture in small increments into molds. "We'll take these to the cellar to cool. Be careful not to spill it."

When they returned, Nancy sat to rest. She poured a glass of water. "Would you care for a drink?"

Veronica shook her head. "All through?"

"No. The kitchen needs cleaning."

"And you expect me to do it? I'm not your servant."

Exhaustion claimed Nancy's gravid body. "I don't expect you to do anything you don't want to do."

"I need to tell you something." Veronica's voice shook slightly.

"What is it?" Nancy sensed tension in the air.

"It's about Jeb." Veronica looked at the kitchen floor.

Nancy tried to keep her voice steady as her heart sank. "What about Jeb?"

"He was wonderful to me when I sprained my ankle. He even came to school and helped me teach until I felt better."

"Jeb is a considerate person." The ways he had helped with Tommy flashed through Nancy's mind.

Veronica's voice lowered until it was barely above a whisper. "I've been trying to make time with him." She fluttered her eyelids. "I might be living at Jeb's place soon if things go the way I want them to."

Nancy didn't want to show her feelings, but she couldn't help sighing heavily. She had no right to claim this wonderful man. "Uh…"

"I thought you'd understand. You being married to Amos, and he may come back home any time. And all that. And you look awful."

Nancy rested her elbow on the table and her chin in her palm so Veronica couldn't see her quiver. After a quiet moment, she stood. "I'll go find Peggy Harter and tell her she can make her souse now."

"I'll see if Jeb is working in the smokehouse." Veronica beat her out the door.

Chapter 22

The morning after the hog killing, Nancy sat on the side of her bed and waited until the room stopped spinning. *Can't jump up too fast. Have to avoid getting dizzy.* For this day, she dressed in her loosest dress, the wine-colored one trimmed in ecru lace. She planned to love this all-day social. Nobody, not even Veronica or the Ku Klux Klan or Felton Oglethorpe, would have the power to break her mood. Hair piled in a bun and face powdered, she approved of the way she looked in the mirror.

"Good morning, Mama." In the kitchen, Tommy placed cutlery on the table. "Why you dressed up?"

"It's an important day. Folks are coming from miles around to our get-together." She spread her hands wide.

He turned his head and twisted his mouth. "What do I have to do?"

Nancy coaxed the fire in the stove. "After breakfast and barn chores, wash your face, put on your best school clothes, let me comb your hair, smooth your coverlet on your bed."

"Aw, Mama." He slammed a fist on the table.

"Young man, watch your temper." She reached for her biscuit making supplies and equipment. "Come sift the flour."

As he worked, he mumbled, "My friends won't be dressed up."

"I didn't say dress up. I'm telling you to clean up." She kneaded the biscuit batter. "Son, today when you see all the good friends we have and enjoy the tasty food, you'll be proud you're an O'Reilly."

He scowled. "I'm not proud to be an O'Reilly because Xan Miller told everybody at school Papa deserted us."

She sliced ham and placed it in a skillet. "He doesn't know that. He said that so other boys and girls would think he was smart. Your papa didn't desert us."

"That means something bad happened to him."

She rolled the biscuits out and placed them in a pan. "Let's have a good time today with our friends. We don't know what happened to Papa. We do know he'd want us to enjoy our party."

Tommy set four plates on the table.

By the time the biscuits browned, Jeb popped through the door with Evie. He placed her on her high seat and poured drinks for all. Coffee for Nancy and himself, milk for Evie and Tommy. "As soon as Tommy and me finish the farm chores, I'll start organizing things in the yard."

Nancy served the biscuits with ham. "You look nice today, Jeb."

He laughed as he brushed his shoulders. "I'll try to stay clean."

After breakfast, Nancy did the dishes. Then she gave Evie a quick wash off and helped her into a clean dress. Tommy returned and got himself ready. Jeb went to work in the yard. By the time they finished preparing, the guests started pulling into the yard.

Friends from church arrived in noisy groups piled into wagons with their neighbors. Folks came from everywhere throughout the community. The ones who lived close by walked.

The guests from farther away let their mules into her paddock or took them to Jeb's pasture. Drivers pulled up to her porch to let the riders out, then went to find places to park their wagons. It was more than she could keep up with.

Women placed cakes and pies on the tables. Some brought jugs of cool sweet tea. Nancy's kitchen buzzed with cooks baking sourdough rolls they'd made at home and brought in pans, women chopping cabbage for slaw, and others peeling potatoes. Men helped carry warm pots of beans to the stove. Nancy arranged slices of her hogshead cheese on a plate.

Some women even brought plates, utensils, and cutlery from home. Children ran everywhere playing games and yelling with excitement. Since this Saturday was chilly, everyone bundled up. The meal would be served outside at the picnic table, on the porch, or on the tails of wagons.

Laughter punctuated loud talk throughout the house and yard until a hush fell over the crowd as Jeb, Harold, and Steve opened the pit and removed the pig, along with pork butt roasts placed beside it. The smoky aroma wafted through the air. They used all sorts of platters and pans to hold the tender meat as they chopped it and pulled it into bite-sized pieces.

The guests oohed and aahed.

Jeb laid down his carving knife and fork. "Brother Barlow, would you say grace?"

When the pastor finished, the crowd roared, "Amen."

Food adorned tables throughout the house and front yard, and the guests went from one spot to another until their plates were piled high with deliciousness.

After the meal and a minimal amount of cleaning, some of the men filled the pit with wood, and blazes leaped up. Folks stood around warming their hands as the fire flickered and danced, causing faces to glow. Women brought blankets and quilts from their wagons.

Jeb stationed himself by the picnic table, which was a comfortable distance from the fire. He tuned his guitar. Nimble fingers produced soft chords that modulated into the melody of "Amazing Grace." His rich baritone voice projected into the afternoon air as he sang the first verse. The guests joined in to produce an emotional rendition of the popular hymn, verse after verse.

Veronica, wearing her hair tied back with a yellow ribbon and dressed in a blouse with a plunging neckline, prissed in front of the group as she dragged a chair from the kitchen. While she placed her chair, she leaned forward toward Jeb. To the beat of the music, she swung her head. Nancy looked past Veronica.

"Evie, your papa sings and plays pretty music." Nancy snuggled the child. Tommy, having spent hours playing with his friends, came and sat by his mother.

Jeb sang and played, "Precious Lord, Take My Hand." The visitors joined in.

He strummed chords. "Come up here, Nancy."

Nancy stood and wobbled toward him, Evie pulling on her leg and Tommy holding her hand.

"Sing us a verse of it."

She lifted her rich alto voice. "Hold my hand, lest I fall."

The song continued with verses repeated, the music going on and on. Jeb set his guitar down and addressed the group. "Would some of you share a few stories with us?"

Folks recalled happy childhood memories and told their hopes for the future. "When the railroad comes through here, we'll have a town close by."

As the time together passed on, a hush fell over the crowd. Jeb picked up his guitar and led the neighbors in "Shall We Gather at the River?"

He laid the instrument back down and motioned a question to Nancy with his hands. *Time to end the party?*

A thrill went through her when she realized she and Jeb communicated without words. She smiled and breathed "Yes."

"Friends, help us eat up this food. Come get some more to munch on now and take all you want home with you." Jeb's voice carried throughout Nancy's large front yard.

A wave of confusion brought her remorse. She'd waited week after week for Amos to come home. After the magnificent party, she found it more difficult than ever to back away from the sweet friendship with Jeb.

As the sun slipped behind the trees, the men claimed their mules from the paddocks and hitched them to the wagons.

Veronica stepped over to the Bynums' wagon. "Y'all go on. Jeb will take me home."

Evie reached toward Nancy's arms, and Jeb lifted his daughter. "Go ahead," he said to Veronica. "I need to stay and help."

Veronica, her lips pouting, climbed into the back of the Bynums' wagon.

The party ended soon after the sun disappeared beyond the horizon. The wagons, full of laughing and singing passengers, departed. One wagon came toward Nancy's house though. Felton drove up to the place where Jeb gathered dishes from the picnic table.

"Evening, Felton." Jeb laid down the dishes and looked up at the owner of the mercantile.

Nancy stepped forward. "We can still fix you a plate."

Felton slurred his words. "I ought to shoot you for taking all my customers away. Why did you have the party on a Saturday?"

Jeb spread his hands open. "It was a good day to have it."

Felton looked all around. "Where's your dog?"

Nancy pointed toward the front yard. "Not here."

"Then it's safe for me to get out of my wagon." Felton, staggering, tripped on a rock, and a flask fell from his shirt pocket.

Jeb lifted Felton to a standing position and took him over to lean against his wagon. Slowly Jeb eased him to the open back of it and seated him there.

"Felton, you're as drunk as a fiddler." Nancy piled food on a plate for him. At close range, the smell of soured corn whiskey on his breath gagged her. "Eat something. It'll help you sober up."

He pushed the plate away. "I don't need anything to eat."

"Oh, come on." She placed a smoked rib in his hand.

He let it slip through his fingers. "I just want…" He fell backwards.

"Looks like he's passed out." Jeb removed a small pistol from the pocket of Felton's trousers.

Nancy raised an eyebrow.

"He said he should shoot me. So I'm disarming him."

"What are you going to do with him?" Nancy asked.

"Nothing."

"You can't just do nothing. He'll wake up in the middle of the night and come after me."

"Let me think. What if I take him to my place?"

"You can't do that either. He may shoot you and Evie when he wakes up."

"But I have his gun." Jeb flashed the pistol. "What do you want me to do then, Mrs. O'Reilly?"

"Push him up into the wagon. His mules will take him home."

Chapter 23

Felton drove his team to his usual parking space next to Jeb's spot and tethered his team to a low limb. He pulled his hat down over his bruise.

"Good morning, Felton. How did you get a black eye?" Nancy made a point of sounding sympathetic.

Jeb, you're chicken. Keeping yourself out of sight by checking on your horses.

Felton cupped his hand over the injured eye. "Blankety blank robbers."

"Oh, no." She was glad he didn't curse, although she considered him a hypocrite for cleaning up his language simply because he was on the church grounds on Sunday. "What happened?"

"They knocked me over. I fell and hit myself on something sharp." His gray green eyes pierced into hers as if he hoped for some evidence she believed him.

"Who?" Did he try to see if she believed him?

All shifty-eyed and fidgety, Felton ignored the question.

You don't remember what happened, do you? Now you have to make up something.

"What did they steal from you?"

He spoke in a singsong voice. "My pistol and all the money I had in my wallet."

Nancy willed herself not to smile, and she was careful not to make eye contact, although Felton leaned over toward her.

Felton makes me want to laugh with his stupid lies.

"Did you see them? Who were they?"

Felton paused. "Well, actually, it was only one robber. I seen him. B. K. Barnes. He pushed me down."

"Really?" She worked hard not to laugh. B. K. and his family could have arrived in Chicago by then.

After church, Nancy and Jeb returned to her house to eat leftovers. As soon as he took Evie home, Nancy, in her favorite spot on the front porch, relaxed in the afterglow of Saturday's get-together as Tommy played in the front yard.

The only thing that could have made Saturday's roasted suckling pig celebration better would have been Amos's return. She told herself she wanted him to come back, but her fantasies confused her. What if he'd left her? What if he had another family in a neighboring town? If he'd been murdered, she needed to know so her mind could have peace.

Jeb, with his helpfulness, constant attention to her needs, guitar playing, and manly good looks, made it difficult for her to mourn appropriately. He was a temptation. She indulged in tender feelings, unsuitable for a woman expecting a child and missing her husband.

Reflections about Jeb provoked dreams she couldn't allow herself to have. What really mattered for her was being a good mother. Tommy needed a happy home, Evie called her Mommy, and the new baby would soon become her greatest responsibility.

When the weather warmed after the cool spell, Nancy had a sudden burst of energy. It would be fun to make a black walnut cake using Granny's recipe. The walnuts had fallen weeks earlier. Their outer husks had turned yellowish green and become soft, but she hadn't managed to harvest them. Now they were dark brown, almost black. If they stayed on the ground much longer, they'd develop mold.

What would it hurt if she picked them up from the ground and placed them in Tommy's little red wooden wagon that Amos made for him last Christmas? There was leftover red paint in the barn storehouse. The walnuts probably wouldn't stain the wagon, but if they did, she'd brush on another coat. To protect the wagon's finish, she decided to layer the bottom with a croker sack.

Nancy had a serious plan to gather some walnuts, but she didn't know how she'd manage if she had Evie with her.

She wanted to enjoy the sunshine before the cold weather settled in. And to indulge in the beauty of the farm as much as she could before her confinement. Thanksgiving was the fourth Thursday of the month. Her baby was due in a few weeks, maybe after the first of December. She wasn't sure about the day.

There would be time before Thanksgiving for the nuts to dry. She'd ask Jeb to crack them with a hammer so she could pick out the delicious nutmeat.

Thursday was a warm golden morning. Jeb turned to her before taking Tommy to school. "I won't leave Evie with you today. We're going to ride into Mize to shop. The weather's nice. We won't have many more days like this."

She beamed at him. He'd worked all week on finishing his house, and he needed to take a break. "Have a good trip."

He pushed a stray strand of her hair into place. "I'd invite you to go with us, but the road's too bumpy for you."

"Do you need me to pick up Tommy after school?"

He sighed. "We should be back in time, but you never can tell what might happen."

Nancy laid her hand on Jeb's arm. "When you get back, come by here and let me know. If you don't show up by two o'clock, I'll go for him."

Jeb placed his hand on top of hers. "I'll do my best. I wouldn't want you to have to hitch up the mules as far along as you are."

"I can walk him home from school."

"Yep. The road isn't boggy, but climbing the big hill could tire you out."

After Jeb left with Tommy and Evie, Nancy tied on her bonnet and donned a lightweight coat. "Come on, Grover. Let's go for a walk in the woods. What a marvelous day to be outside."

Along her path, late-turning foliage hung in sprays of color as brown leaves dropped in the light breeze. No matter how pleasant the day, dangers still lurked. She watched for things that moved or blended into the background. Instinctively she sniffed for the smell of snakes. "Grover, we have to watch our steps."

They traveled on the path next to the Mize road, the way Amos used to take most times. An impressive black walnut tree stood on the side of the trail. A substantial limb hung over a bed of sand where she'd be able to find enough walnuts without having to dig around in the briars on the other side.

Before she picked up any walnuts, she stood underneath the tree and toed the sand. Memories of the times when Amos had brought Tommy here to play flooded over her. It was the period before Amos started working away from the farm. Life was easier. How she had begged him to stay at home and not work at the mill.

Nancy doubted she'd go out walking this far many times before the baby was born. This adventure was hers to enjoy, a special day the Lord had given her.

Peggy Harter's cousin Iris, a midwife, would come and stay with her and Tommy after Thanksgiving. Then, Nancy would have to do exactly what she was told. Today, however, she was free.

The tree had shed its broad leaves. She selected a few walnuts, but she didn't pick up too many and make her load heavy. As always, she studied the ground carefully for reptiles, such as snakes, also lizards. As she collected the walnuts, she constantly looked a few feet ahead of herself for any potential trouble. The recent winds had rearranged the sand beneath the tree. In a new low place, she saw some hard objects.

Limbs from the tree?

No, they were light gray, almost white.

Bones!

Maybe an animal died there. A frayed rope lay among the bones.

Human bones!

The other end of the rope hung tied around a large branch. A human skull lay in the pile. A money pouch left open. And there were shoes. The remains of brogans. Amos's money pouch. Amos's brogans.

Amos!

Nancy collapsed. When she recovered from fainting, she experienced the sensation of a contraction. Empty handed, she wobbled toward her house.

The contractions persisted, not strong yet, but unmistakable. She made it home and sat leaning backwards in a chair on the porch.

At one o'clock, Jeb returned and put Evie down for a nap. He rushed back to the porch. "You're awful quiet. You're shaking all over, and you're pale as a sheet."

She spoke in a hoarse whisper. "The baby's coming."

"What did you say?" His voice trembled as he started down the steps. "I'll go get the midwife."

"The midwife isn't coming to visit the Harters…oh." Her breath caught as she strained. "Until after Thanksgiving."

"I'll go get somebody." He bolted toward the wagon. "You need help."

"Don't leave me." She pleaded, "Come back."

"But -" Jeb turned toward her and stood wringing his hands.

"You'll have to help me." She grimaced with another contraction.

"I think I'm supposed to boil water."

"Go ahead." She gasped. "But as soon as you get the fire going, come on back."

He went to the kitchen, started the fire, washed his hands, and returned. Then he laid his hands gently on her shoulders. "Tell me what to do."

"The baby's coming fast. Help me turn around in the chair."

"Grover, get off the porch." Jeb scolded the dog. "Sorry, boy. We don't need your help. Go chase a rabbit."

Grover tucked his tail and slinked underneath the house.

Jeb repositioned her. "Now what?"

Nancy emitted an ear-splitting groan. "Catch it."

"Catch her." He yelled. "It's a girl."

The newborn let out a robust cry.

Throughout the delivery, Evie didn't stir from her nap.

Following Nancy's instructions, he tied the cord with rags cleansed in the boiling water, cut the cord, placed the baby to nurse, and assisted with the passing of the afterbirth as she directed. The smell - sour, sweet, and earthy - pricked his nostrils.

Nancy looked into Jeb's face as he gazed down at her. "I found Amos."

"Do you know what you said?"

"Yes."

"You're sure you found Amos?"

Exhaustion overwhelmed Nancy. She closed her eyes and spoke softly. "I'll tell you about it later."

"Try to rest, Nancy."

"Tommy must have gone home with Veronica after school."

Chapter 24

Jeb didn't know what to do next, but he felt he could do anything now that he'd delivered a baby. His chest puffed out in triumph as tears stung his eyes.

"Get a blanket and throw it over us." Nancy shivered as a sudden autumn wind whistled through the trees. Whorls of leaves found their way onto the porch.

"Don't fall asleep 'til I come back." He touched the baby's back and brushed his hand over the mother's cheek. Then he raced to Nancy's room and yanked a soft blanket off her bed, along with the afghan from the rocking chair.

Back on the porch, he wrapped the mother and new baby gently.

"Tired…so tired…" Nancy fell asleep.

Would she drop the little girl? Jeb reached for the baby. *Got to wrap her up.* He knew how to hold her so her head wouldn't flop around. With one hand placed under the infant's head, he enveloped her in the afghan. His heart swelled within his chest. Jeb extended a finger to touch her tiny hand. "I love you, little baby girl. You're beautiful."

He planted a feather-soft kiss on the baby's cheek. *I'll always take care of you and love you like you're my own. No matter what happens, you'll be Evie's little sister as far as I'm concerned.*

Nancy lay sprawled in the chair behind him. *Thump.* Was she falling?

No, it was just her feet landing on the floor. *Nancy, I'll be right back. Please don't fall.* He placed the baby in the middle of Nancy's bed and spun around toward the front porch. Nancy's eyes were rolled back, and her hands fell limp beside her. "We've got to get you in bed."

"Yes." Her voice quivered as she leaned on him and tried to stand.

"Easy." He scooped her up into his arms and carried her.

Evie slept on.

"You're sopping wet." He found one of her gowns. "The baby's in the middle of your bed. Can you stand there and hold on to the bed post 'til I can help you change?"

"Be careful." Nancy warbled when she spoke.

"I will."

As he removed her sticky wet clothes, he forced himself to keep his eyes on the baby.

Nancy stood shivering, her hands reaching out. "Quick. Hand me the gown."

He kept his eyes pointed toward the baby as she pulled the gown over her head.

"Let's get you in bed now."

"No." Nancy's voice was weak but emphatic. "Pad the bed with towels. Put the baby in the cradle."

Jeb hit his forehead with his palm. *Why didn't I notice the cradle?*

After he fixed the bed, he took Nancy's arm and wrapped it around his neck. "Hold onto my shoulder."

When she lay in bed, he took the baby from the cradle and placed it in the crook of Nancy's arm.

Evie wandered into the room.

Thank you, Lord, for small favors. Jeb bent down toward his own little daughter. "Look, Evie. Miss Nancy has a new baby."

Evie held up her delicate little hands for Jeb to pick her up, and he lifted his daughter. He leaned over so Evie could get a close look.

"Ah, pretty baby."

"Yes." Jeb beamed. "She's beautiful. She has blonde hair like you, Nancy. Her little face is perfectly shaped."

"She's precious," Nancy whispered. "Where's Tommy?"

"Veronica takes children home with her if their parents don't show up. He'll be all right."

But how and when could Tommy get home? He needed someone to show up and stay with Nancy and the new baby.

Tommy burst into Nancy's room. "Did y'all forget me?"

The teacher, followed by Steve and Jenny Mae Bynum, rushed into the room after Tommy.

Nancy extended her hand across the bed toward Tommy. "No, son. We didn't forget you. Our baby came."

Tommy slammed his elbows into his chest as he whined, "Why didn't Mr. Jeb come for me then?"

Jeb tousled Tommy's hair. What words would the six-year-old understand? How much did he know about such things?

Nancy's voice sounded tender. "He delivered the baby."

Veronica's mouth flew open. "You delivered a baby?"

Jenny Mae leaned forward. "I would have helped."

Since Evie was squirming, Jeb lowered her to the floor.

Tommy took her hand. "Come on, Evie. Let's find the molasses teacakes."

Jeb nodded toward Jenny Mae. "We didn't have time. The baby came fast."

"Would you like for me to help you get cleaned up and wash the new little one too?" Jenny Mae inched toward the head of the bed.

"I'd love that. Wash her first. She has plenty of clothes in the top drawer of my bureau."

Jenny Mae lifted the baby carefully.

While Veronica, Steve, and Jeb stood around, Jenny Mae bathed the newborn, who screamed and turned red at being disturbed from her comfortable spot beside her mother. Jenny Mae cooed to the infant and soothed her. "You're a perfect little girl. I can already see you're going to be strong-willed though."

Jenny Mae passed the baby, now diapered and wearing a soft white gown, to Jeb. "Y'all, step out of here so I can help Nancy get cleaned up."

In the kitchen Jeb poured milk for Tommy and Evie. "This is a special day. Tommy, you are blessed to have a new sister. Evie, you have a new friend. Let's all work together to take care of this precious gift from God."

Big eyed and silent, the children laid down their cookies and looked up at him.

As Veronica handed them their milk, she gazed at Jeb with melancholy eyes.

"Here's the family Bible." Steve removed the leather-bound book from the shelf.

After Nancy's bath, everyone but Tommy and Evie returned to the bedroom, and Jeb brought the baby back to her. "I think she's hungry."

As Nancy took the baby to nurse, Jenny Mae handed her a receiving blanket to use as a nursing cover.

Jeb couldn't take his eyes off the mother and baby. "What are you going to name her?"

"If you don't mind, I'd like to name her Mary Ann after your late wife."

The tears that Jeb had held back all afternoon streaked down his cheeks. "I'd love that."

Steve held the Bible. "Nancy, would you like for me to record the birth of Mary Ann O'Reilly in your family Bible?"

"Yes, please. Look on my writing table for the quill and ink."

Steve pulled reading spectacles from a case in his shirt pocket and perched them on his nose and ears. When he sat and dipped the quill in the ink well, he turned to the page between the Testaments. "Spelling, please."

Jeb looked at Nancy. "Ann without an *e*, right?"

"If that's the way your wife spelled it, then yes." Nancy patted the baby softly. "O'Reilly with one *e*."

Steve spelled the name before he wrote it. He fanned the ink with his outstretched hand.

"Don't close the Bible." Nancy raised her head from her pillow and propped up with her free arm. "Under the section that says 'deaths,' record Amos O'Reilly's name."

Steve sat up straight and looked at her over his glasses. "Really?"

"Yes. Write his name and today's date. Then add 'Remains found.'"

Jenny Mae brought her hands to her mouth and rushed to the head of Nancy's bed. Veronica ran out of the room. Jeb blinked his eyes.

"Where's Tommy?" Nancy looked around.

Jeb stood at the foot of Nancy's bed. "He and Evie are playing in his room."

"I'll have to tell him this soon when we're by ourselves." Nancy laid her head on her pillow.

"Take your time." Jenny Mae smoothed the bedcovers.

A hush fell over the room. Nancy closed her eyes and breathed slow sighs of fatigue. Jenny Mae lifted baby Mary Ann from Nancy's arms. "Let's try out the rocking chair."

The men tiptoed to the kitchen.

"Steve, you've done so much for me already, but I need to ask one more thing." Jeb swallowed hard. "Could y'all stay a few more minutes while I tend to the stock and milk the cows?"

Steve slapped Jeb's back. "I'll be glad to. In fact, I'll come help you. Where's Veronica?"

They found her sitting on the porch. "Veronica, I'm going to help Jeb with the farm chores. We'll be here a few more minutes. Could you keep an eye on the children?"

Veronica, face blotched and tearstained, turned toward the men for an instant. Then she looked away. "No. I'm going to walk back to your house. I need to clear my head."

"So be it." Steve went to the door of Nancy's room. With whispers and gestures, he asked Jenny Mae to watch out for the children. "I'm going with Jeb to the barn."

As the men performed the evening chores, Steve talked about Veronica. "She's unhappy teaching. She wants a family. Soon after the school term started, she got a letter saying her true love had married someone else."

"Sounds like trouble."

"She's had her sights fixed on you, if you haven't noticed."

"I've noticed, all right."

"When you helped her with her teaching after she sprained her ankle, she told us you had taken a shine to her."

Jeb shook his head and chuckled. "If she thought that, I'm sorry. I just saw she needed somebody to help her."

They finished the O'Reilly chores and returned to the house. Jenny Mae was firing up the stove. "Give me a few minutes, fellows, and I'll cook us up some supper."

"Sounds good," Jeb said. "Why don't I go over to my place and do my farm chores?"

"Let's go." Steve followed him out the door.

After the Bynums left and bedtime came, Jeb read a story and a Bible verse to Tommy and Evie. He put Evie to bed on her pallet in the corner of the kitchen.

When he went to check on Nancy, she sat rocking the baby.

He kissed little Mary Ann's forehead. "I'll sleep on the front porch."

Jeb reclined on a pallet. The wind caused the trees to drop more leaves. Somewhere nearby an animal released a musky smell. Farther away the coyotes called to one another. In her own time Nancy would tell him how she found Amos. He wouldn't rush her. He needed more than anything else to rest. *Dear Heavenly Father, thank you for…*

His prayer trailed off.

The next afternoon while Tommy was at school and Evie was taking her nap, Jeb sat in a chair near Nancy and watched her rock the baby. "Talk to me about finding Amos."

Nancy told him the entire story. "I'm eager to recover his bones before some animal totes them off, but I realize they've been lying in that spot for months."

"Sunday, I'll arrange for the church deacons to help collect the remains. We'll construct a pine box to place them in."

"Amos will need a proper funeral and burial. The box can be small, no more than something to hold his bones. The O'Reilly plot is to the west of the magnolia tree."

In the moments before he needed to bring Tommy home from school, Jeb took a shovel to the walnut tree and heaped a mound of sand over the exposed bones.

Veronica had dreamed of a future with Jeb, but she could see he didn't have any romantic interest in her. What hope did she have for a satisfactory life in this God-forsaken piney woods with little connection to the outside world? It was a community without a name. The train didn't go through it, and it had only one store.

Friday evening, she packed her trunk. "I can't take this any longer. Drive me to Mt. Olive tomorrow to catch the train."

Steve Bynum looked at her with wide eyes. "What about the children?"

"I don't care. I'm not cut out to be a teacher. Last night when I decided to leave, I thought I'd go back one more day to be sure."

"Do you know what time the train goes through?"

She rolled her eyes. "I don't care about that either. I'll wait in the depot until it shows up. All I want is to get away from here."

Steve released a heavy sigh. "Sleep on it another night, and maybe you'll see it differently tomorrow. Think about all the advantages of being a teacher."

She held balled-up fists in the air. "If you say one more thing like that, I'll find somebody else to give me a ride. I'm leaving. Don't you understand?"

Chapter 25

Nancy wasn't sure how long Jeb had been rattling pans in the kitchen. He must have gotten up extra early to milk and do the farm chores. Biscuits and bacon for breakfast were warming on the stove.

She'd slept short periods throughout the night between nursing the newborn baby. Nancy didn't hear him leave with Evie. When they returned, Evie wore one of her new dresses, and her hair was combed. Jeb looked sharp in his Sunday suit.

"You're working too hard." Nancy talked to Jeb while she rocked Mary Ann on the front porch. "You tend to your chores and mine. Take Tommy to school. Help cook the meals. Wash clothes. Hope to find a chance to work on your new house. And when you tended to your farm animals, I suspect you toted Evie the entire time. It's too much. And you've slept on this porch for three nights."

"It's okay." He stood in the doorway. "Come on, Evie. Let's see if Tommy needs any help getting ready to go to church."

"Thanks for taking him."

Tommy stepped onto the porch.

"Wait a minute, son. I'll comb your hair." While Jeb parted the boy's hair with a wet comb, he gave Nancy some instructions. "If you think about it, check on that pot of beans I put on the stove for lunch. Are you sure you'll be all right here?"

"We'll do fine. We'll go inside. I'll keep my pistol and shotgun handy." She hugged Tommy on his way to Jeb's surrey.

"That's right. You shoot like Annie Oakley." He winked at her. "And a right smart prettier."

Soon after they left, Nancy laid the baby in the cradle with a gentle motion.

When did I last fix my hair? Nancy looked at herself in the mirror. *What a mess!* She braided her hair, washed her face, and quickly bathed herself in the basin. She found a soft, flowing blue housedress, tied a matching blue ribbon to the end of her braid, and smoothed a tiny bit of beeswax on her face to give it a glow.

Jeb placed the children in the back seat as he did when Nancy rode with them. He missed her lovely presence as he drove the short distance to church. On the first day Jeb saw her, he suspected her husband had gone and would not come back. Their connection had consisted of two lonely young neighbors who faced the forceful tide of life without mates. Two parents providing material and emotional support for their children solo. Two farmers determined to survive in a remote southern frontier.

As the months passed, he'd wanted to wrap his arms around her, tell her that he'd take care of her, and give her comfort as she spent the lonely nights in the isolated countryside. If he'd had a weaker sense of morality, he would have rushed into the situation. He dared not tread on dangerous ground, not because he was afraid of any man. Instead, he didn't want to tempt her to violate her commitment as long as she hoped her husband was alive. He feared breaking God's laws.

Now that the evidence showed she was a widow, he'd give her time, but how much time would she need? His goal was to make her want him. He'd show his love by taking care of her and the children. And he wanted to move their relationship to a new level, a feeling of love. Jeb would look for ways to romance her.

Before he left North Carolina, he assembled his resources. His family had left him enough money to build a comfortable home. Since arriving in Mississippi, he'd used the funds frugally while he worked hard and accepted the help of others to build a suitable home for him and Evie. His whitewashed house had glass windows, two fireplaces, and a cooking stove.

He'd saved enough to buy seeds and fertilizer so he could plant the fields in the spring. Jeb would plant Nancy's crops whether or not anything more developed between them than friendship.

As soon as he tethered the horses in the spot where he usually parked, he inspected the children and helped Evie jump to the ground. Seated in church with one child on either side of him, he prayed to the Lord for guidance.

On the way home, Tommy asked, "Mr. Jeb, what do you do?"

"I'm a farmer."

"When you're not farming, what else do you do? Are you a carpenter?"

"Yes. That's what my father did. He taught me how to hammer and saw when I was no bigger than you."

"My papa and I used to make blocks. I like to cut and saw wood."

"Yes. I've seen those blocks on the porch."

Tommy placed his hand on Jeb's shoulder. "Will you teach me carpentering?"

Jeb felt a twinge of remorse that he hadn't already started teaching the boy. "Sure thing."

"I can work with you like Arnold and Matthew did."

"When you're not at school, I'd love for you to help. Son, you've been going through some tough times. Losing your pa, and now your mama's having to spend most of her time with the new baby."

Tommy sniffled. "I can handle all this."

"I know." Jeb paused. "It will be a good thing for you to help me with carpentry work. I'm glad you've already had experience."

Jeb's mind drifted. He believed that someday soon the railroad would pass nearby. They lived in the midst of a wealth of virgin timber. He'd never go off to the mill the way Amos did, but in the late fall and winter after he harvested his crops, he could find work building whatever village might develop. That way, he'd provide for Nancy, himself, and their children. He savored the dream of their future.

The moment Jeb returned with Tommy and Evie, Nancy stood in the doorway. The children bounced over to her with hugs.

"We had a good time, Mama." Tommy beamed up at her and went inside with Evie.

Jeb stopped near her and took her hand. "You look rested. It must have done you good to have a little while to yourself."

"Yes."

He hugged her lightly. "You're supposed to take it easy for a few days. Come on to the kitchen and talk to me while I make cornbread."

She poured a glass of water and sat.

He removed his coat and loosened his tie. As he rolled up his shirt sleeves, Nancy found herself admiring his powerful shoulders and muscular arms. *Jeb McAllister, you are a handsome man.*

He mixed the ingredients for cornbread and cooked it on the stove. "I'm going to make a pone. That's a quick way to do it."

"Okay. Granny used to make it that way."

He let the cornbread cook until it rose high in the skillet and was brown on the bottom. Then he turned half of it over onto the other side.

"That's a pretty crust. It's going to be delicious." The aroma of the bread cooking made Nancy hungry. "You're a good cook."

"And you are a beautiful woman. Do you know that you have me under your complete control? All you have to do is beam at me with your lovely eyes the color of the sky."

"Aw, Jeb." She picked at him. "Really?"

When they finished eating, Tommy helped Jeb wash the dishes while Nancy sat in the rocking chair on the porch and nursed the baby.

A few minutes later, Jeb came outside. He turned a ladder-backed chair upside down and lay down with his head propped up on the back, even though he wore his best shirt. "We won't have many more days like this before cold weather sets in."

Tommy and Evie took little buckets to look for treasures in the yard.

"Felton." Nancy shielded her eyes with one hand to watch him drive his wagon up to the front of her porch. "What brings you out this Sunday afternoon?"

"Come to see the new baby."

Nancy stayed in her chair but held Mary Ann up for him to take a look.

Grover barked and jumped toward Felton, who moved to the center of the front of the wagon. "Call off your dog. If this keeps on, somebody's going to poison him."

Jeb stood, bringing the chair with him. "Afternoon, Felton. If anybody poisons Grover, I'll come looking for you."

"You don't have to get huffy. I meant it as advice."

Jeb frowned. "Keep your advice and threats to yourself."

"Who says I have to? I have another recommendation for you."

Jeb ran his fingers through his hair. "Oh?"

"If you don't start spending more time in that nice new house you built, somebody's going to burn it down."

"Where I stay is my business."

"Nancy, it took you long enough to find out where Amos died." Felton lifted his reins but called his team back. "Whoa. I was about to forget to give you this here letter."

Jeb went down the steps and snatched the letter from Felton.

"Careful there. You wouldn't want to tear it."

"Thanks." Jeb took the letter to Nancy.

Felton slapped the reins and headed out.

To my dear sweet Nancy,

Hope this letter finds you and yours well. Sold the place. Your pa and I got loaded up in the wagon to come live with you. Took what I could, but since he needed to rest because his lumbago bothered him, the mattress took up most of the space. Have a fine team of horses.

We took off early one sunny morning. Right when we got to Fayette, your pa grabbed his chest and breathed his last. Let me assure you that he didn't suffer.

Turned around and took his remains back to Port Gibson. Some dear friends let me stay at their lovely home. We gave him a nice funeral. Too bad you didn't get to be there or to see him one last time.

Still hoping to get to your place before the cold sets in.

Love,

Granny Willietta

Nancy read the letter silently, then handed it to Jeb, who read it aloud.

He jumped up. "See you in two or three hours."

Leaving Evie to help Tommy look for treasures, Jeb ran toward his house.

What was that about?

When he returned wearing his overalls, he called Tommy. "Let's go do our barnyard chores."

Nancy stirred up the fire and added fresh wood to the stove. Since she felt good, she had no trouble cooking a pile of hotcakes for supper.

As they ate, she watched Jeb. "What did that letter say that put you in fast motion? You were already working every minute. You know you're supposed to rest some on the Lord's Day."

"I rested long enough." He buttered his cakes and poured molasses on them.

"What's happening?"

"Your granny could show up any time. We have to get ready."

Mary Ann cried. Nancy took her from the cradle and brought her to the kitchen. "I know, I know. I need to finish cleaning out the spare room. I will when I get the time and energy."

Jeb finished his stack of pancakes and ate the ones that remained on the platter. "What you need to do is rest more."

"Sometimes we have to exist in peace no matter the circumstances." Nancy frowned as she tried to affirm a feeling she didn't have.

"Don't worry about it, Nancy. I'll help you."

"You need to work on getting your house finished and set up." She gave him a pleading look. "When will you have time?"

"I'll make time."

"Oh, by the way," she said. "You don't need to sleep on my front porch. We'll be fine."

Monday morning when Jeb took Tommy to school, Jessie McCleskey stood at the doorway to greet the children. She wrung her hands. "I'm no teacher, but Miss Veronica up and left Saturday. I'll fill in until they find somebody qualified."

Jeb shook his head. "Oh, no. I thought she'd make a good teacher when she got some experience."

Back at Nancy's house, Jeb loaded into the Harters' wagon with the deacons and rode the short distance to find Amos's bones underneath the black walnut tree. When they approached the pile of sand, they hopped out of the wagon. Jeb removed his hat and bowed his head. "It's sad."

The others also stood in reverence, heads bowed and hats in hands. Harold Harter prayed.

They collected Amos's bones and dropped them into burlap bags which they loaded into the wagon. Harold said, "We'll keep them at my house because that's where we'll build his box."

Deacon Smith studied the bags. "The box don't need to be more than four feet long, but we should make the coffin as nice as possible. Amos was a good man. He worked hard to provide for his family. We need to show Nancy our respect."

"No." Harold shook his head. "We ought to make it a full size so folks can remember Amos O'Reilly was a tall man."

They dug around until no more bones remained. Shovels piled into the wagon, the men loaded up. Jeb sat on the tail of the wagon, his feet dragging the ground. "What would be a suitable occasion to lay him to rest?"

"Sunday after next when the preacher's here ought to be good." Steve Bynum said. "Jeb, you could ask Nancy if she's okay with the time."

Harold clucked to his mules. "The women will cook up a good meal. If the temperature don't drop off before then, it'll be the last time we get to eat on the grounds this year."

In the meantime, Jeb paid an unexpected visit to Nancy's house one afternoon. "I'm here to help you finish cleaning out the spare room. You never know when you'll need it."

Chapter 26

A team of palomino horses, golden with creamy manes, pulled a wagon into Nancy's yard. The driver sitting erect on the bench looked tiny, hardly five feet tall. Her hair, a mixture of black and silver-gray, was pulled in a tight bun at the nape of her neck. The woman's bonnet hung on her back from cloth strings. Her no-nonsense expression and her high-necked long-sleeved gray dress gave the impression that she meant business.

It had been eight years since Nancy saw her grandmother last. Nancy remembered her looking taller and having black hair. The same stern expression had not changed.

Within reach, a rifle lay waiting. Nancy supposed the wiry little lady kept it handy, should she need it. And a feisty little white dog with a patch of black hair over her left eye yapped from the side of the wagon.

Nancy, with little Mary Ann in her arms, jumped up from the porch rocking chair. "Granny!"

"Hey, Nancy." Granny stopped her team. "Hush your barking, Dolly."

The dog paid no attention but went right on barking.

"Come tie your horses." Nancy pointed toward the hitching post by the front porch.

"Can't wait to see the wee one." Granny, spry as a thirty-five-year-old, stepped from the wagon.

While Granny tethered the horses, Nancy pulled the cover back from baby Mary Ann's face.

"She's a fine looking little one. I'll get a better look when she wakes up."

Nancy reached to hug Granny. "I'm so glad you came."

Granny looked all around. "Where's Amos?"

"Amos passed away." Nancy choked on the words. With her free hand, she opened the door for Granny. "Somebody murdered him."

"Oh, that's a shock. You've got to tell me all about it."

"I'll tell you what I know so far." Nancy placed cold biscuits and ham on a plate for Granny. "You hungry?"

"Starving, child."

Nancy poured a glass of cool tea and a glass of buttermilk.

"I've got so many questions. Is this Amos's baby? How long ago did he die? Have you gotten married again, or are you living in sin?"

Despite the gravity of the circumstances, Granny's questions amused Nancy. She laughed. "No, I'm not living in sin. This is Amos's baby."

As soon as Granny scarfed down the food, she stood. "I need to take the horses to your watering trough."

"Let me show you where it is. After they take a drink, you can turn them into my paddock. The branch runs through it if they get thirsty again."

As Granny busied herself with the horses, Nancy strolled back inside to check the spare room. A comforter and pillows with shams looked inviting. The room had a bureau. A desk with a lamp on it and a chair in front of it waited for Granny.

Jeb blesses my life every day.

Granny unpacked the few belongings she had.

"That mattress I have in my wagon has seen better days."

Nancy grinned to keep from insulting her.

"I was hoping to throw it away." Granny sat on the bed, and Nancy sat in the chair.

"Give me the baby." As soon as Nancy placed little Mary Ann in Granny's arms, Granny laid her on the bed. "Tommy at school?"

"Yes."

"I so want to see him."

"When Tommy comes home, you'll get to see our friend Jeb and his little girl Evie too."

"Great. How's Tommy doing in school?"

"You know he's in first grade. Tommy's a bright little boy, but he got off to a slow start. His teacher didn't do much, and she left. Now a friend of mine tries to teach the children, but she doesn't know anything about being a teacher."

Granny sat up straight. "How'd you like it if I took over the teaching job in Tommy's school? What would the other folks think?"

Nancy brought her hands together. "I'd love that. Everybody in the community would love it. Don't take on too much, Granny."

"After what I've been through nursing your pa and driving across the state by myself? Teaching a few boys and girls would be a picnic for me."

Chapter 27

When the Sunday of Amos's funeral came, the church overflowed with friends from throughout the community. At the front of the church stood the coffin, a masterpiece of woodwork. A white pall lay over the closed box.

As Susanna Barlow, the pastor's wife, played "Softly and Tenderly" on the piano, Nancy sauntered in with her loved ones to the front pew. Dressed in black, she jiggled baby Mary Ann. Tommy sat close to her, their expressions fixed like stones. Next to Tommy, Granny Willietta found her place. She lifted her head high with a dignified expression. After Granny, Jeb toted Evie and seated her on his knee.

Nancy experienced deep grief blended with a sense of relief that Amos was finally having a proper burial. Deacon Harter spoke the eulogy, and Pastor Barlow read holy words of comfort from the Bible. Nancy looked sideways toward Jeb. Tears streamed unbidden down his face. *What a tender heart!*

At the end of the service, Miss Susanna played "Rock of Ages" for the pallbearers to lift the coffin and take it out of the church and for Nancy to walk out followed by her family and Jeb's family. Next Miss Susanna modulated into "Abide with Me" as the congregation filed out of the church and followed Nancy to the freshly dug grave next to Amos's parents in the

O'Reilly section. It was in the back of the cemetery west of the ancient magnolia.

Across the split-rail fence, giant hardwood trees that had lost their leaves stood thick. The wind, brisk and unrelenting, whistled through their branches. Nancy shivered as she covered baby Mary Ann's face with a blanket.

Jeb placed a supportive hand on her waist and guided her to the bench beside the grave. After Nancy stationed herself on the bench and pulled Tommy and Evie close, Jeb assisted Granny to walk across the uneven ground and reach the bench.

Granny placed her hand inside the crook of his elbow. "Thank you, young man. I'll sit here."

Jeb stood behind Nancy.

The pastor read a Psalm and said another prayer. Men lowered the coffin into the ground. As shovels buried Amos's remains, a long line of friends came to give Nancy gentle hugs and admire the baby. Their sweet words ran together in her mind. Oh, to be able to remember what everyone said.

Granny reached out to everyone who passed in front of her. She repeated each person's name and looked into their eyes. With her youthful attitude and concern for others, Granny Willietta gave Nancy's heart a reason to sing.

"I've missed you, Granny."

Walking to the front of the cemetery, Nancy held the baby securely, Jeb supported Nancy with his left arm, and Granny clasped his right arm. In her other hand she held Evie's hand. Tommy held Evie's other hand.

Jeb hovered over the group as they selected food. Granny helped Evie with her plate. They stationed themselves at the surrey. Jeb ate while Nancy nursed the baby. Then he took her in his arms so Nancy could eat. The way Granny bonded with Evie and Tommy amazed Nancy.

After the meal, the congregation went inside the church. Nancy led her group to the front, where the pastor stood. She handed her baby to the minister. Mary Ann continued to rest peacefully as Brother Barlow's voice resonated throughout the sanctuary.

"Beloved friends, we will now dedicate this precious daughter of Amos and Nancy O'Reilly to the Lord. In our children lies the promise of a brighter tomorrow." He looked toward Nancy. "By what name is this child to be called?"

"Mary Ann O'Reilly."

He prayed in a gentle voice:

Our most gracious Heavenly Father, we ask you to bless Mary Ann with health, strength, and courage. As she grows up, may she be a shining example of your love. Teach her to know your grace. Be with her always and keep her from harm.

It is my prayer that all who are present will help her grow close to you as she matures. In the name of your Son, Jesus. Amen.

He strolled from the front of the church to the back and returned, with the baby's face showing. "Allow me to introduce you to Mary Ann O'Reilly."

He handed the baby back to Nancy and led the worshippers to stand and sing "Jesus Loves Me." As Nancy departed with her family and the McAllisters, she thought nothing could go wrong that day until…

She looked into the scowling face of Felton Oglethorpe.

Back home, Nancy, after all the feelings she'd experienced that day, needed to take a stroll so she could sort things out. "Granny, if you're not too tired, would you mind watching the children a few minutes while I take a walk?"

"No, you go on, girl. I suspect we'll all take a little snooze."

Jeb had gone to turn the horses into the paddock.

Nancy wandered toward the Cohay bank. A crisp breeze caressed her face and unfurled her skirt. The soft steady sound of the rushing water never stopped. No matter what each day brought, her life went on like the creek until it reached its destination. She knew the Cohay's waters rolled toward the

Leaf River, but where the events of her life would take her she didn't know.

For months, she'd fought the feelings within her heart - wrong emotions because she wasn't sure until a few days ago that her beloved Amos would never come back. Now, she could allow herself to love this man, but only if she knew he loved her. He'd kept his distance. Was it because he was a gentleman, or was it because he didn't have any romantic interest in her? If she were a more brazen woman, she'd ask him.

Nancy stood listening to the birds and to the sound of the singing creek.

"Hi."

"Oh!" Nancy jumped. "You frightened me. I'm glad it was you."

"I confess I followed you because I wanted to make sure you were all right."

She grinned at him. "I'm fine."

"This is a beautiful place."

"It's where I like to go to think."

He stood so close she could feel his warm breath. With his calloused hands, he cupped her face and pulled it upward so their eyes met. "May I kiss you?"

"Please."

Jeb leaned toward her and looked into her eyes with tenderness.

When did she last breathe?

His lips brushed along hers softly as she closed her eyes. The kiss removed any doubts she had about whether he loved her. Whatever trials lay ahead for them, they would be able to conquer together. Since he loved her, nothing else mattered. All she could sense was his embrace.

A warmth spread throughout her body.

He pressed his lips against hers, gently at first, then with passion. "I love you, Nancy. I want to spend my life helping you through whatever obstacles you may face."

"I love you, too, Jeb." Her voice soft as a whisper.

They gazed into each other's eyes. With an embarrassed chuckle, she brought her mouth close to his. After one more kiss, one not to be forgotten, he took her hand as they walked back toward her house.

Someone crossed the path in front of them on the way home. Nancy squeezed Jeb's hand as she whispered, "Did you see that?"

Chapter 28

Jeb enjoyed Granny's help, but he felt that he sometimes took advantage of her. Saturday morning was such a time. He gazed down at her with a boyish grin. "Granny Willietta, could you watch the children for a few minutes? I need to take a walk with Nancy so we can discuss some things."

"You go right ahead. Glad I can help out."

Nancy grabbed her sunbonnet. "I promise we won't be gone long."

Jeb and Nancy followed the path to the creek. As soon as they were out of sight, he took her hand and pulled her into the shadow of a live oak tree. He pushed her bonnet back. With his hand cupped around her face, he pulled her into an embrace.

After they shared a few kisses, she took his hand and pulled him toward the creek. "Let's go for a walk."

They climbed down the steep bank and kicked their feet in the sand. "It's too chilly today to take off our shoes."

The white grains glistened in the bright sun. Nancy knelt and lifted a shiny object. "What's this?"

She held it up so the light would shine on it.

"A pretty rock."

"It sparkles like a diamond."

"Let me have a look." He took it from her hands and rolled it over in his palm. "Think I'll keep this."

"Jeb!" She took a petulant tone. "I found it."

He held it out of her reach. A mischievous grin spread across his face. "Thank you. I'm keeping it to remember this walk."

"If you insist." She stirred in the sand. "I'll find another one."

They looked but didn't find one like it.

Almost noiseless waves rippled through the creek. Nancy whispered, "Indian braves."

Jeb kept his voice soft. "Cherokees lived near us in North Carolina."

"A few Chickasaws live along the banks of the Cohay. We have a peaceful co-existence with them."

"Good."

"It's a rumor that Chickasaws are living in the Barneses' cabin."

Hand in hand, Jeb and Nancy strolled up the path.

When Jeb went home, he pulled out a small tin where he kept valuable items along with worthless keepsakes. He pulled out the jewelry that he'd given Mary Ann. Eventually he'd give

Mary Ann's ring, brooch, and string of pearls to Evie. These things were not suitable to give Nancy. He dug around until he found his pa's gold cuff links and necktie pin.

Sunday before church, he pulled Steve Bynum aside. "Do you ever make any jewelry? I thought since you were a blacksmith, you might."

Steve's eyes sparkled. "As a matter of fact, I do. My grandfather taught me blacksmithing and silversmithing. He showed me how to work with gold too."

Jeb pulled the gold pieces and the stone out of his pocket. "I was wondering if I could hire you to make a ring for Nancy."

"I'd be delighted to." He shook his head and waved his hand. "No charge, though."

"Then I don't want you to do it." Jeb sounded stern. "A workman is worthy of his hire. Plus, I want this to be a gift from me to Nancy."

"Oh, all right. Since you put it that way." He reached for the pieces. "Let's take another look at the stone. Where did you get it?"

"Nancy found it on the sandbar of Cohay near her house."

"Quartz. I could cut it and polish it up so it will look like a precious stone." Steve put the stone and gold jewelry inside his money pouch.

"It will be precious to me and Nancy," Jeb leaned his head to one side. He had an earnest look on his face. "When would you be able to make the ring?"

"Oh, I don't know. I'll work on it when I can." A smile burst out and covered Steve's face. "Is there a special occasion?"

Jeb looked off into the distance as he stuffed his hands in his pockets. "Might be."

"When do I need to have it ready?"

"I can't say. I haven't asked her yet."

"We're going to be late for church, and them women will fly out here like a bunch of turkey hens." Jeb pointed at the door. I'll come over to help you on your house starting in the morning."

They hightailed it into church.

Monday morning as Jeb and Steve worked, Jeb said, "How are you going to know what size to make the ring?"

"You'll have to tell me."

Jeb drew a line on a piece of wood. "I don't know how to measure a woman's finger."

"Bring me her ring."

"The one Amos gave her?"

"Yes."

"She's quit wearing it, and this needs to be a surprise."

"Easy." Steve held the wood for Jeb to saw. "Steal the ring."

When the men took a noon break to eat at Nancy's house, Jeb slipped into her bedroom and rummaged through her jewelry box until he found the ring.

Steve sat resting on the front porch as he waited for Nancy to call them to eat. Jeb joined him. "Here it is."

"Good." Steve slipped it onto his little finger. "I'll make a mental note of how far it will slide on comfortably. Now, put it back where you found it."

As Jeb tiptoed toward Nancy's room, she collided with him on her way to call the men to the table. "What are you doing?"

Jeb looked sheepish. "Oh, nothing."

"It sure looks like you're up to something." She went to the porch. "Steve, dinner's served."

Jeb hurried to put the ring back in its place. *Whew.*

While they walked back to Jeb's house after lunch, Steve said, "You gave me more gold than I'll need. I can make you a ring too."

"That would be perfect."

The two men worked every minute they could spare, and by the end of the week, the house neared completion. Jeb placed a hand on Steve's shoulder. "I'll be forever grateful for the help you've given me finishing the house."

"That's what neighbors are for."

Jeb had developed a deep friendship with Steve and hoped to return the favor. "Now, what can I do for you?"

Steve put away his tools. "You don't have to do anything, but if you insist on giving me some assistance, you can come over and help me repair my fence so the cows won't get out."

It was a pleasant December day, one of those times when the weather was cool but not too cold for the men to enjoy working outside. Jeb saddled up Thunder, his pinto gelding, who needed exercise.

He mounted and took off, talking to the horse as they traveled. "You're a funny horse, Thunder. When you're off by yourself, you tend to mosey along, but when you're pulling the wagon beside Lightning, you like to move."

The horse snorted. "What? A horsefly in your face? Nothing excites you much besides horseflies but thunder and gunshots. We ain't expecting either one on this relaxing ride to the Bynums' place."

The bay trees mixed with the hardwoods and pines filled the air with their sweet smell. Jeb found it a wonder that his Maker had scattered such delightful perfume in the woods, where few humans experienced it.

On the way to the Bynums' home, Jeb approached the log schoolhouse. Willietta had the learning situation under control, he was sure. Tommy's progress had accelerated since she'd become the new teacher. Last night, Tommy sat down with him and read a lesson from McGuffey's Reader.

Jeb rode along on Thunder at a calm speed. He'd been taking his life peacefully. He loved Nancy so much that he'd do anything for her, but he didn't want to ask her to marry him until he sensed she was ready. The children brought him happiness. All three of them would one day be his own, and he'd be their papa. What a joy Granny Willietta was!

As Jeb passed the schoolhouse, a man on horseback, his head hunkered down, approached at a breakneck speed.

Jeb steered Thunder to the side of the road to avoid a collision. *Felton Oglethorpe.* Why was he not at the mercantile? Must have needed to see Steve about some blacksmith work.

Since Jeb first settled in the community, he'd sensed that Felton wanted to be an enemy, but Jeb never backed down from the quirky store owner. "Morning, Felton."

Oglethorpe reined his horse in. "Well, we finally meet alone."

"It's a pleasant day. I hope you're enjoying it."

Felton snarled as he pulled his pistol and aimed it at Jeb. "Enough of your small talk. Get off your nag and raise your hands."

Jeb reached for his gun as he dismounted, but Felton yelled, "No funny stuff! If I see your hand moving toward your gun, I won't waste time killing you."

"What's this about, Felton?" Jeb showed his teeth in a forced smile. "Whatever the problem is, can't we discuss it?"

"You already know what the problem is." Felton kept his gun aimed directly at Jeb. "I killed Amos so Nancy would be mine. We hung his body near the house where she would find it and see that she was a widow, but it took her too long."

"Oh, really? You hanged him for his money? I thought you had plenty."

"I shot him. Then I got my gang of KKK boys to hang him and split the money so I'd look innocent. Stop all this talking. Looks like I'm going to have to kill you to get Nancy."

When Jeb lowered his hand to reach for his pistol in its holster, Felton fired. The bullet hit Jeb's arm beneath his shoulder. Jeb collapsed to his knees in agony. Warm blood drenched his shirt sleeve. Although he felt lightheaded, he tried to stand.

Felton leaped off his horse and raised his pistol toward Jeb. "I'll put you out of your misery."

From the schoolhouse, Willietta came flying with her rifle pointed toward Felton.

"Old woman, you've got to be kidding." Felton laughed.

She fired a shot that knocked his gun out of his hand. Both horses bolted and ran away, Thunder toward home and Felton's horse toward the mercantile.

Jeb fell backwards.

"Help me!" Felton placed pressure against the wound in his hand as blood dripped on the ground. Blood darkened his jacket over his belly.

"I'm too busy seeing after Jeb." Willietta pressed against his arm to stop the bleeding.

He heard Tommy. Where was Tommy? His eyes blurred as he looked around. A group of schoolchildren stood in the road.

"Go on away from here. Can't take care of both of you." Willietta told Felton as she pressed Jeb's wound with a cloth.

Jeb winced in pain until his eyes rolled back and closed. The world went black.

Willietta instructed her pupils. "Charlie, run to the Bynums' house and get help. Tell them we need the mister and the missus. The rest of you, go inside and shut the door."

In a few minutes, Charlie and the Bynums came running.

"How can we help?" Steve asked.

Willietta took charge. "Jenny Mae, go with Charlie back to the schoolhouse and watch after the boys and girls."

"Read them a story?" Jenny Mae asked.

"Good idea. Steve, raise Jeb's feet. He fainted."

When Jeb came to, he mumbled, "Take me to Nancy's house. Got to tell y'all something."

Steve hoisted Jeb by lifting his good shoulder and eased him into Willietta's wagon.

Willietta climbed in and resumed her pressure on the wound.

Steve coaxed the horses and caused the wagon to bump on the rough road.

"Go easy. Try not to hit the ruts and jar him again."

Steve slowed the team. "I'm sorry."

"It's okay, Jeb. Rest now. Take it easy." Willietta held pressure with one hand and guarded his head with the other as best she could.

At Nancy's house, Jeb managed to walk up the steps with help from Steve.

"Lay him on my bed." Willietta tossed the sham-covered pillows aside and pulled back the comforter. "Nancy, grab some towels."

Steve positioned Jeb in bed.

"Get my scissors off the bureau," Willietta ordered. "Cut his shirt away from his arm."

Willietta cleaned the wound. Nancy went to the kitchen and returned with a knife and a cup of whiskey.

"Jeb, can you raise up a minute?" Nancy asked.

He managed with his good arm to raise his head and upper body.

Nancy held the cup in front of him. "Drink a swig of whiskey."

Jeb choked and sputtered as he drank. Shivering, he collapsed back onto the bed.

"Steve, raise his feet." Willietta covered him with a blanket.

Nancy talked into his ear. "Jeb, dearest, I hate to do this, but I need to check the wound to make sure you don't have any metal left in it."

"Come on, Jeb. You can do it." Steve placed an old leather pouch in Jeb's mouth. "Bite this."

Jeb opened his eyes for a second. "Uh huh."

Nancy dug through the wound and found a few bits of the bullet. Willietta washed the open place and poured whiskey into it. Next, Nancy pushed the skin together over his arm, and Willietta wrapped it with a white rag.

Nancy spoke softly to Granny. "He needs stitches, but I don't have the skill or equipment. We'll have to keep it pushed together but not tied so tight we cut off the blood supply to his hand."

Granny Willietta held Jeb's hand. "You done good. We're going to get you better."

Steve removed Jeb's shoes. "Looks like y'all have this under control. I need to leave. Got urgent business."

Jeb in a weak voice tried to talk. "Wait, Steve. You need to know…"

Nancy leaned close to Jeb. "Need to know what? Try to tell us."

Jeb took a deep breath and winced. "Felton killed Amos."

Nancy collapsed into a chair.

"He said that?" Steve proceeded to the door. "Got to go."

"Take my wagon," Granny told Steve.

Steve untied the team and climbed in. He slapped the reins as he clucked to the horses. "We've got to hurry."

He drove the wagon to Deacon Harold Harter's house.

Harold darted out the door. "Fine looking team of horses you've got there."

"Holler and tell Peggy we have an emergency. Then climb on in. I'll explain as we go."

Immediately the two men drove to the schoolhouse and toward the mercantile. Steve looked on the left. "Harold, you look on the right. It's doubtful that Felton was able to walk back to the mercantile. He was injured pretty bad. Hand bleeding, blood on his shirt too. Looked like he was in awful pain."

"There." Harold pointed at Felton lying in the road.

"Whoa!"

Harold hopped out and went over to check Felton. "Still breathing."

Steve drove the wagon so the back end was near Felton. "Has the bleeding stopped?"

"I think so. Let's load him up."

Steve moved his lips to say, "Mize?"

Harold nodded.

Willietta's superior team of horses made good time as Steve drove them to Deputy Jones's office. When they arrived, Harold went to the door. "Could you come out here, Deputy?"

Deputy Jones stood and placed his pistol in its holster.

"Harold Harter's my name."

The men shook hands.

"And this here's Steve Bynum."

They shook. The deputy peered into the wagon. "Looks like Felton Oglethorpe, who owns the mercantile down the road. He's injured."

Crusted blood covered his hand. Dark stains spread across the front of his jacket.

"Gunfire." Harold shook his head. "He tried to kill Jeb McAllister."

"I know Jeb. A decent sort of guy. What seemed to be the problem?"

"Felton shot Jeb over a woman."

Deputy Jones grinned. "I stay out of domestic squabbles. Did they shoot each other?"

"No, no, no. The woman's grandmother, Willietta Raymond, shot Oglethorpe in the hand to keep him from killing Jeb. Oglethorpe shot Jeb first, but before that he confessed that he killed Amos O'Reilly. His gang was involved."

"Probably those simpletons Jeb McAllister brought in a while back. They're in the state prison in Jackson. We's got to see about Felton. How long has he been out of it?"

Steve said, "We don't know. We found him like this in the road."

The three of them dragged Felton into the deputy's office.

"We'd best be going." Harold jumped into the wagon.

Steve drove back to Nancy's house. He and Harold went inside to check on Jeb.

Still lying in bed, Jeb looked pale. "It's time for me to milk the cows and see about the stock."

"No, you aren't going into the barnyard until your arm heals." Willietta shook her finger at Jeb. "You don't want to get lockjaw."

"I'll milk and feed the stock." Nancy sat holding MaryAnn.

"Our wives are already worried about us. It won't hurt for us to spend a few more minutes." Harold placed a hand on Steve's shoulder. "Come on, Steve. We'll put up your horses, Miss Willietta, and get Nancy's mules and wagon."

"I know the routine. It won't take long." Steve turned to Nancy. "Do you mind if I bring your mules and wagon back tomorrow?"

Nancy paced back and forth holding Mary Ann. "No, that's fine."

Nancy held a cup of chicken broth to Jeb's lips. "Lucky it was your left arm."

After supper, her gaze met Granny's tired eyes. "Could you do one more thing?"

"Sure. What's that?" Granny's smile deepened the wrinkles around her eyes.

"Could you read with Tommy and Evie, say prayers with them, and put Evie to bed on the pallet in the corner of the kitchen?"

Granny's eyes brightened. "I'd love to."

Nancy laid little Mary Ann inside the cradle and checked on Jeb, who snored softly. He rested peacefully.

She snuggled under her comforter. Granny climbed into bed with Nancy.

Dear God, please watch over each of us. Keep Jeb safe and help him get well soon. Keep his house safe too. Thank you for bringing this wonderful man into my life. And bless my amazing granny. In Your Son's name, Amen.

Chapter 29

Jeb's ragged scar took its sweet time closing. During his recovery, he found solace in Willietta's room. Evie made do with her pallet in the kitchen, while Granny Willietta shared Nancy and the baby's room. Tommy, as usual, remained in his own room. Jeb left the responsibility of guarding his new house within walking distance of Nancy's place to his loyal dog Cleopatra.

"This is some arrangement." Jeb half-smiled as he sat over breakfast with Nancy.

With Baby Mary Ann nestled on her mommy's shoulder, Nancy gently patted and rubbed until the little one released a hearty burp. Nancy's beautiful eyes locked with his as she shook her head. A playful grin burst forth. "How so?"

Jeb leaned in, sipping his coffee. "My house is so close to being finished with plenty of space. Yet here I sit crowding y'all because you and Willietta won't grant me any freedom, not even to go over and feed Cleopatra."

Nancy's grin widened, her eyes dancing. "Well now, you're more than welcome to accompany me to your house and tend to your dog while I check on your livestock. When Granny and Tommy are at school, I'll have to hitch up a team of mules or horses. It's quite a hassle when Granny's not around. I can't take my eyes off you. You'd let Cleopatra lick your wounds."

Nancy jiggled the baby, her voice filled with affection. "We can't trust you to take care of yourself, and besides, we need to dress your wound. By the way, don't use your left arm to lift Evie."

Jeb sighed. "Yes, ma'am."

Nancy made cooing noises to Mary Ann. "I'm so glad Granny came to live here."

Jeb extended a finger, and the baby wrapped her tiny hand around it. Evie held onto Jeb's leg. How could his arm hurt with so much love surrounding him? "Besides half a dozen reasons your granny helps us, one of the important ways is that she guards our reputation. It wouldn't look right having me live here. Our church friends may start to talk about us."

One of the things he loved about Nancy was the way she organized her days. At first he'd found her remarks scattered, but after spending more time with her, he realized she had a dozen thoughts going on in her head at once. He marveled at what she accomplished.

Nancy offered one of her spontaneous remarks. "I've been pondering something. What if we let the young cow dry up? Then we can breed her."

Jeb considered her suggestion. "Good idea. As soon as my arm gets better, I'll take her to spend time in Harold Harter's pasture."

Nancy stood to take Mary Ann to her cradle for a nap. "What would we do if it weren't for our neighbors?"

"You and me need to bake something for early Christmas presents." Jeb refilled Nancy's coffee cup as a bashful grin spread across his face. "I know how to make buttermilk pie."

"You're serious?" Her eyes grew big with a look of disbelief.

"Absolutely. When I fix it fancy, I dress it up with pecans on top. How many pie pans have you got?"

"Five."

"Excellent. I'll make pies for four families - Harold Harters, Zach Smiths, Steve Bynums, and Stu McCleskeys."

Nancy winked at him. "And one for us?"

"Of course." How sweet she looked.

By midafternoon, they'd cracked and picked out a large bowl full of pecans. Jeb propped his left arm on the table. "Sorry. I can't do much of this."

"Stop then. We have almost enough." Nancy moved his pan of cracked pecans out of his reach, her warm fingers touching the top of his hand.

"Yes, ma'am." He helped Evie take care of her doll. "Do we have all the other ingredients we need?"

"Buttermilk. What else?"

"Flour, lard, sugar, eggs, butter." Jeb checked Nancy's supplies. "You've got plenty of eggs and butter, and I have flour, lard, and sugar at my house."

"I've got some nutmeg you could season the pies with."

"Interesting. Also, I'll go with you over to my place this afternoon and find the vanilla flavor."

"Mmm. Sounds good." Her eyes lit up.

The following day dawned with Jeb's hand poised to create special gifts for his neighbors. He maneuvered his left arm and hand as little as possible and relied on his right hand for the strength he needed. Meanwhile, Nancy kindled the fire to heat the oven, swept up flour, and wiped the work areas clean.

Since Jeb had been trying to use his left arm as little as possible, his muscles ached when he used the rolling pin. He worked diligently, doing most of the work with his right hand, as he rolled out the crusts, which showed evidence of his years of practice. He doubted that other men in the piney woods of Mississippi knew how to make pie crusts, or if they did, they wouldn't admit it. Then he mixed the filling and poured it into the pie shells.

Nancy examined the pecans to remove any chaff they'd missed, and he sprinkled the nuts on top. By midmorning, the pies, all golden brown, cooled in a row while the filling set. The aroma of the freshly baked goodness filled the air. Memories of his childhood carried him to a time when his mother taught him the skill of baking pies.

"They're perfect." Nancy inspected each pie. "I'd planned to keep the worst looking one for us, but they all look marvelous."

His heart swelled at her wonderful compliment. He couldn't help but smile.

Since it was a nippy day, they bundled up in their light coats and hats. Evie touched her pink cap and placed her fingers gently on Mary Ann's matching cap. "I've got a hat just like Maywee Ann's. We sisters."

Jeb spoke tenderly to her. "Miss Nancy made those for you and Mary Ann."

Evie shook her head. "Don't call her Miss Nancy. She's my mommy."

Nancy harnessed Jeb's horses to the wagon and maneuvered it to the parking spot near the front porch. After they made the girls presentable and tidied their own appearances, they carefully loaded four of the pies on dishcloths atop freshly laundered bath towels into the wagon. Mindful of his arm, Jeb gingerly climbed in.

"Can you hold Mary Ann?" Nancy handed the little bundle to Jeb.

"Sure." He cradled Nancy's baby with tender love, as if the infant were his own.

Nancy helped Jeb's sweet little daughter Evie climb into the wagon and followed. Evie nestled in her snug spot between them.

"Grover, stay." Nancy took the reins and assumed control of the horses. They embarked on the pie-delivering journey without pausing for visits.

During the return trip to Nancy's house, Jeb was drawn to her gentle presence. She possessed a natural beauty that rivaled that of any woman he had ever beheld. Her warmth. Her beautiful blonde hair escaped from her bonnet and blew in the breeze. Her sky-blue eyes sparkled with unspoken thoughts. Despite the chill of the day, she didn't wear gloves on her calloused hands, which were in constant motion. Nancy had not been granted the luxury of delicate, pampered hands, but the love that flowed through them possessed a rare and exquisite allure.

"Nancy." He spoke her name as if he had something important he needed to say. He'd wanted to wait until his arm healed, but he couldn't contain his feelings another minute. "Will you…" He had to get this right. "Will you honor me by becoming my wife?"

She didn't speak.

Dear God, will Nancy turn me down?

The sounds of the horses' hooves clicking in rhythm on the solid ground, the occasional creaking of the wagon wheels, and the fluttering uncertainty within his chest - these were the only sounds he heard.

Nancy, say something!

Did she fear he'd never be able to work again because of the injury to his arm from the gunshot wound? Would she find it ridiculous to marry him and risk having another baby in a few months?

How he'd hurt inside if she laughed at his earnest request. Maybe she found it peculiar that they rode down the road with two little girls, one his own and one Nancy's, with her having to drive the team. In this atmosphere that lacked the grandeur of romance, he had emotions in his heart that surged forth and took over. He anxiously awaited her reply.

With her face turned toward his, she finally spoke. "Marry you?"

He wondered whether he'd ever love her more than he did that moment, and yet she tortured him by leaving him to guess what her answer would be.

"Yes, will you marry me?" He had to let her know how he felt. His gaze met hers. With a steady voice, he tried to explain his feelings. "As soon as my arm heals, I want to make you my wife. I love you, dearest Nancy, with all my heart." He softly laid his left hand on hers while being careful to hold the baby with his right hand.

The horses picked up their speed, as if they sensed the joy in the air. Evie laughed, and for the first time, Mary Ann chortled.

For Jeb the moment felt as though it stretched into eternity as if time stood suspended. She had spoken nothing, but the joy of love filled the air. Still, he needed her to tell him....

"Marry you?" She said the words again in a soft, tender tone.

His heart thundered within his chest like the clamor of a thousand drums, while his spirit sang like an entire orchestra.

Nancy, tell me.

She kept him hanging in suspense as she drew out the moment. Time lingered, as their gaze locked, the moment being stretched as in an endless song. A deep breath escaped her lips, and he echoed her sigh.

"I love you, too, Jeb." She breathed the words he longed to hear in a voice that reminded him of a tender melody sung by reeds in the wind. "You've shown me a love that lights up my heart. Through all that's happened in the last few months, you have been a source of strength for me. Whatever lies ahead, we'll face together." Her voice reached a determined crescendo. "Stop worrying about your arm. It will heal in time. Let's have a Christmas wedding."

Relief washed over him like cleansing waters. *Thank you, Lord, that we will be a family.* He fought back his tears of joy.

Ignoring the lingering soreness of the gunshot wound, he reached out to her cheek with a delicate touch. His loving smile brought a tingle to his lips.

As she pulled back on the reins, she slowed the horses almost to a stop.

Taking care to hold Mary Ann securely, he leaned over, closing the distance between them. Evie, having fallen asleep, rested her head on Nancy's lap. Jeb found Nancy's lips and kissed her to seal the flame of the love burning between them.

Theirs would be a family with a future of promise, enough to last a lifetime. Hand in hand, they would conquer any obstacles that lay ahead.

She slapped the reins. "I can't wait to tell Tommy and Granny Willietta."

Chapter 30

Willietta's weary back ached all across her shoulders and below her waist too. Her legs cried out in distress. She'd never let a little problem like pain in her muscles and joints stop her from doing what needed to be done. That morning, as soon as she stepped out of bed, she'd slathered on Nine Oils Liniment, which she'd brought from Port Gibson for herself and her horses. Since it was impossible to reach all the way behind her, she ignored the backache...or at least tried to push the discomfort aside.

Christmas, with all its warmth and significance, approached fast. Joy filled her heart. As she taught the children their parts for the Christmas program and guided them through rehearsals, she felt a sense of anticipation. Who knew how many more Christmases she'd celebrate on this side of heaven? What a delight to have one more opportunity in her life to teach another year! She didn't see this coming, and she'd never let on to Nancy or Tommy or that fine young man, Jeb McAllister, that she had trouble putting one foot in front of the other at the end of each school day.

She knew how to make the children laugh as they learned. Her pupils' spirits soared like ornaments hung on a Christmas tree. After practice, she introduced a new task. "Now, my dear boys and girls, we'll make paper chains." Her eyes twinkled. "We'll add a touch of magic to our tree."

None of the boys and girls complained about having to be in a school room with children of different ages. As a seasoned teacher, Willietta enjoyed finding activities that required various levels of skill.

She showed them how to make ornaments by cutting paper. "We ought to save this paper to write your lessons on. It's hard to come by, you know, but the grace of Christmas comes only once a year."

Meanwhile, Zach Smith, who had three children attending the school and a warm heart full of the Christmas spirit, donated a magnificent cedar tree to Miss Willietta's students. Its branches touched the ceiling and spread throughout a corner of the schoolroom.

"Mighty fine, Mr. Zach. That there tree's got the schoolhouse smelling like cedar."

The boys and girls left their desks to gather around and watch. They took deep breaths to sniff the smell that announced the approach of Christmas.

He put on his hat and coat. "What else can I do for you, ma'am?"

"Do you have a sturdy ladder? Would you be so kind as to bring it tomorrow?" She had no plans to climb it herself, not with her aching back. If he brought it though somehow the top of the tree would receive its share of ornaments, including the big star the older students had constructed.

Early the following morning while Willietta stoked the fire in the pot-bellied stove so the room would be warm when the children arrived, the three Smith children burst through the door. Zach followed, carrying his stand-up ladder. Peter, his youngest child, asked, "Teacher, are you planning to climb the ladder and hang the chains on the branches?"

She placed her hand on her hip. "I know my limits. My back has bothered me as of late. I could ask my big boys to do this but what if they fall?"

It was a free-standing ladder. Zach placed it in front of the tree. "It looks like it's my job."

"Mighty fine."

He went to work hanging the chain. Miss Willietta couldn't resist the urge to stand in a chair near the back of one side to pass the rope around. She called Charlie, the tall, older boy, who'd helped with other shaky problems, like the time he ran to get help when Jeb got shot. "Stand in a chair on the other side."

When they finished, she wagged a playful finger at Charlie. "Now, remember, young man, don't let me catch you standing on a chair again."

Charlie's eyes widened. His mouth flew open. "But -"

"Charlie!"

He nodded earnestly and flashed an innocent smile. "Yes, teacher. I promise not to stand on chairs again."

Throughout the schoolroom a spirit of Christmas joy filled the air.

The Saturday of the party arrived. It was a splendid December day, cool and clear. Willietta, in a voice full of anticipation, asked Nancy to take her and Tommy to school early.

"I'll hitch the team to the surrey." Jeb started toward the door.

"You can help, but I'll need to make sure you don't hurt your arm." Nancy hovered over Jeb. "Could you keep an eye on the children? This won't take too long, Granny."

"That'll be good. I'll get myself ready to go."

A few moments later, she took Granny and Tommy in the surrey to school. Nancy tethered the horses. "Let me start the fire in the stove. You look so pretty, Granny. You don't need to get dirty."

Tommy paced about as he rehearsed his lines.

Nancy checked him over. "I'm so proud of you, son."

"Thanks, Mama."

"I'll go get Jeb, Evie, and Mary Ann."

Willietta checked all the details of the schoolroom. *I hope the program and party will bring the spirit of Christmas to every person who comes here.* She'd cleaned the books off her desk the day before. One last minute detail remained, spreading a starched and ironed white tablecloth over her desk.

"Tommy, this is a big boy job. Come stand on the side of my desk and help me with the tablecloth. Don't dare drop it."

Immediately after they positioned the cloth on the makeshift table, the room began to fill with students accompanied by their parents and grandparents. Platters of delectable cookies found their way onto Willietta's desk.

Each student brought a gift prepared and wrapped by family members. The fathers tied the smaller packages to the tree and placed the larger ones on the floor in front of it. The children too young to attend school had their own gifts lovingly wrapped and waiting.

The fathers and grandfathers, along with some of the mothers, stood, tall and erect, their eyes beaming. As Willietta searched their faces, she was delighted to see the parents showing love for their children. Some of the mothers and grandmothers who could not stand for an extended time nestled in the pupils' desks. Nancy, holding little Mary Ann in her arms and keeping Evie close by in a small chair, settled to rest and enjoy the festivities. Willietta stationed herself in a chair to the side of the area she called the stage.

When the program began, Tommy took center stage. Evie stood on her chair and called out, "Tommy."

A titter passed through the group. Tommy cleared his throat and in a pure and innocent voice initiated the recitation of "'Twas the Night Before Christmas." Willietta was glad she had selected him to start the program, not because he was her great grandson, but because the words danced on his tongue.

The other primary students continued with their solo verses, and at the end the entire group recited in unison.

Next came singing. The younger children, their voices like tinkling bells, sang joyful Christmas songs, including "Jingle Bells" and "Up on a House Top." Their eyes twinkled as they sang beloved Christmas carols.

The older students moved to the front of the group. Johnny Harter's rich, young voice led off with the recitation of Luke 2. The older students joined in reading the story of Jesus' birth. The presentation was as sincere and profound as Willietta had hoped it would be.

After they finished, she rose from her chair and motioned to Jeb, who walked around the edge of the audience and brought his guitar out of the coat closet. She helped him put his strap around his shoulder in a position that didn't bother his arm.

"Now, it's your time. Mr. Jeb McAllister will accompany us as we sing 'Silent Night.'"

The radiance of Nancy's face changed to a bright glow of anger. Why did Nancy frown? Willietta had expected her to be delighted with the surprise, but no.

At the end of the reverent delivery of the lovely hymn, which had recently become popular, one of the fathers stoked the fire in the pot-bellied stove. Others lit kerosene lamps.

A sudden hush fell over the group as children looked toward the door. Santa Claus, laughing and wishing everyone, "Merry Christmas," burst through the door. He wore a bright red suit and had a flowing snow-white beard. His eyes twinkled. It took quite a while for him to distribute the gifts.

The children played with their toys. The family members talked nonstop. Soon all the cookies disappeared.

At the end of the party, Miss Willietta looked for a chair. "I'm all tuckered out."

Nancy didn't smile as Jeb came to stand by her and take Evie's hand.

"You didn't like our little surprise, did you?" Jeb's grin was full of mischief.

"Why didn't you tell me?"

"You would have been afraid I'd hurt my arm, but I was careful."

"So, you kept it a secret that you were playing your guitar again. You and Granny."

Chapter 31

After all the other parents had departed, Nancy addressed Jeb in a testy voice. "Would you please go out to the surrey and get some quilts so the children can take a nap while we clean up?"

Her eyes burned as she spit out her words, but Jeb responded in a soothing voice. "Sure, I'll be glad to."

She swished around helping Granny set the schoolroom back in order. "We need to sweep up all this food from the floor. If we don't, vermin will take over the place."

"Slow down some." Granny held a hand on her back as she tried to wipe away the crumbs on the pupils' desks. "Stop your fuming."

Mary Ann cried when Nancy tried to lay her on a pallet. Evie kicked and whined in the fussiness of a tantrum. "Can we go home now?"

Tommy, his head downcast, picked up wrapping paper from the floor and placed it in the trash can.

Nancy's heart thudded as she grabbed the straw broom so she could sweep up the clutter. *Some people are so inconsiderate. If they would pick up after themselves, there wouldn't be so much left for us to clean.* She felt worried lines etch across her face. She fussed to herself. "I don't know why Granny doesn't wrap her broom tighter and tie the string."

Evie tugged at Nancy's skirt.

"Jeb, do something with this child." In a brisk motion, Nancy continued to sweep.

Jeb called Evie to him and led her over to a quilt folded into a pallet. "It was a good program, and you got to see Santa Claus. Here's your new dolly. I think she's tired. Could you snuggle her and hold her so she can get a little nap?"

The scene touched Nancy's heart, but she was still angry. How could he risk messing up his arm?

After they put the room in reasonable order, Jeb approached Nancy. "I'll take Granny and Tommy home. Then I'll come back for you and the girls."

"All right." *Maybe you'll cook up another scheme between here and the house.*

Jeb told her, "Latch the door from the inside."

"Okay."

Nancy sat locked inside the school room with Evie and Mary Ann. Evie sat beside Nancy and rested against her. Mary Ann awakened with a cry of hunger. When Nancy positioned the baby to nurse, nothing worked right. After a moment, Mary Ann cried a loud angry squeal.

Nancy swung the baby in her arms as she prayed. *Lord, I try to be strong no matter what. For the moment though, I'm weak. Please help me to overcome my anger toward Jeb and Granny. Hold me in your arms as your child so I can care for these precious little girls.*

Give me the right words to say to my sweet husband to be and my amazing grandmother. Help me to show Tommy how much I appreciate him. Let me speak and react through your strength, since I've used up all I have.

Thank you for these moments to collect my thoughts and cool my feelings. In Christ's name, Amen.

She tried again to nurse Mary Ann. The baby settled in contentment.

The familiar creaks and squeaks of the surrey accompanied by the horses' hoofs hitting the hard dirt came closer. "It's Jeb," he called to her, his voice coming to her through the gentle breeze like a tender whisper.

Holding Mary Ann and nudging Evie along, Nancy inched her way to the door and unlocked it.

Jeb rushed inside and gazed at her with sad eyes, his lips forming a downward curve. Remembering her prayer, she yearned to reach for him. Her pride said she wasn't ready. They needed to talk.

Instead, she stood before him with her attention focused on the girls. The surroundings, so full of the noisy mirth of soon-to-come Christmas, now looked tired as silence weighed heavily on the deserted school room. Neither of them spoke a word as Jeb checked the stove and made sure the window shutters were locked. He turned down the wicks of all the lights but one lantern, which he carried with him.

Holding Mary Ann, Nancy made slow progress walking to the surrey as Evie pulled her skirt.

He secured the lamp on a lantern hook at the front left side of the carriage and went back for the quilts as Nancy loaded Evie and climbed in, still holding Mary Ann. *Loading two little ones is quite a feat.*

Since the darkness of night fell with only soft moonlight and the lantern to guide them, Jeb coaxed Thunder and Lightning to step gingerly. He spoke to the horses and to Evie, but not to Nancy.

She wasn't ready to say the words that would have torn down the wall between them. Misery took charge of the moment, which threatened to last forever.

Jeb must have felt like this when I took so long to answer him the day he proposed. And now we're having our first misunderstanding.

She gave him a tentative pat on his shoulder.

He drove to Nancy's front porch, stepped out, and tethered the horses to her hitching post. With his right arm, he helped sleepy Evie out of the surrey. While he led Evie inside,

Nancy maneuvered her way out of the surrey as she held the baby. He returned, and she handed Mary Ann to him and unhitched the horses. She tied Thunder to the hitching post and led Lightning toward the paddock. A soft glow approached her from behind. Jeb must have placed the baby in the cradle and come back to hold the kerosene lantern to light her path.

"Thank you," she said.

Then they went back for Thunder, Jeb's gentle gelding, and placed him in the paddock.

Halfway back to the house, Jeb hung the lantern on a post and reached for her hand. Without taking the time to talk, he wrapped her in his right arm and pulled her to him in a firm but gentle embrace. She turned her face up to him, and he kissed her as a man starved for love.

She lost herself in the kiss. In sweet surrender she let go of her worries and fear, her resentments and disappointments, all the negative thoughts that made barriers between them. The passionate kiss reminded her that their love ran deep like mighty waters.

"We'd better go." She reluctantly pulled away.

He reached for the lantern. "Yes. Granny Willietta will be worried about us."

They rushed along, hand in hand. Back in the kitchen, Tommy was setting the table. Granny sat in one chair, her feet elevated in another. Rubbing her eyes, Evie sat on her pallet in the corner.

"I've got hot biscuits waiting on the stove and some fried ham." Granny looked away from Nancy.

"You must be awfully tired. You didn't have to do that." Nancy rushed to hug her grandmother, but Granny shrugged her shoulders.

"Somebody had to." Granny pointed to the plates. "Help yourselves. We need to eat so these tired young'uns can get to bed."

Over the meal, Jeb announced, "It's time for me and Evie to move back to my house. My arm is well enough."

"It isn't completely healed but go ahead." Nancy didn't protest.

After supper, Granny yawned. "Sorry, folks. I'm leaving it with you."

"I'll join you soon," Nancy called.

Jeb rolled up his sleeves. "It's my turn to wash the dishes."

Nancy reached for her Bible. "So, it must be my turn to say prayers with Tommy and Evie."

The house settled into quietness except when the wind blew in bursts that made the boards creak and the tin shingles rattle. Nancy threw an afghan around her shoulders, then opened the front door with as little noise as possible.

Soon after she seated herself on the front porch, Jeb, wrapped in a light blanket from his bed, joined her in a nearby chair. "As I said over supper, it's time for me and Evie to move back to my house."

With one hand, she wiped the tear that slid down her cheek. With the other, she reached for Jeb's hand.

He laced his fingers in hers. "Dearest." His voice was softer than a whisper. "I'm sorry for not telling you I was playing my guitar again. I thought I could handle it, but if I'd mentioned it, you would have insisted playing would pull on my scar. If it had caused me any pain, I would have stopped. Besides, playing in the program meant something to Granny and the children."

She squeezed his hand and let go. "And we've tried to help you keep it from getting infected. I feel a little silly, but I've tried so hard to help you heal that arm." Her voice quivered. "No more surprises, Jeb. Promise?"

"I will not. I love surprises, and sometimes it's my way of showing how I care for you." He stood and offered her his hand. "Come here."

Holding on to their wraps, they strolled to the steps and to the other side of the surrey. She giggled. "Are we taking a trip?"

He pulled her into his arms and brushed a kiss on her lips. "Yes, love."

They climbed into the back seat. Snuggled close, they indulged their hearts in the warmth of their love. She whispered, "We're being unconventional."

They shared a slow deep kiss.

She pulled away to breathe. "I'm so in love with you, Jeb McAllister."

His voice grew husky. "Nancy, I'm ready for our wedding day."

She pecked his cheek. "I think it's time to go back inside."

By her bedroom door he kissed her one more time. "Good night, sweet Nancy."

She opened the door and shut it softly to avoid disturbing Granny. Catching her breath, Nancy brought the top of her hand to her lips.

As if she suddenly remembered where she was, she tiptoed over to her gown and changed for bed.

After Nancy climbed into bed, Granny stirred. "Nancy, my dear girl, I never meant to upset you. I thought it would be a delightful surprise for you and everyone at the program."

Nancy reached over to Granny and planted a kiss on the older woman's cheek. "I'm sorry I overreacted."

The elderly woman drew in a labored breath.

"You all right, Granny?"

"Tired. My legs and back are complaining because I worked them too hard."

Nancy left the bed and fumbled around with no light except the moon shining through the windows. "Here's the witch hazel cream. Let me rub your feet."

Granny kicked the comforter off and instantly relaxed. "Jeb McAllister is a good man. You and him make old love new again."

"Do we remind you of when you were young and Grandpa was alive?"

"Yes, honey child, but he went off and got shot in the war."

Nancy finished massaging Granny's feet and ankles.

"Rub that cream on up to my knees. My calves are killing me."

Nancy rubbed gently. "How about your back?"

"Reach over there and get that Nine Oils Liniment. Would you mind rubbing a little of it on my old back?"

"I'd be glad to."

Soon afterwards, Granny snored. Nancy smoothed her grandmother's gown and covered her with the comforter.

Tired as Nancy was, she stayed awake visualizing the wedding.

Chapter 32

"You do realize we're getting married next Sunday?" Nancy looked anxiously at Jeb. How would they be ready?

"I know." His eyes glistened as he kissed her hand. "I can't wait."

"But, Jeb. We should wear new clothes. We could postpone it so I'd have time to make new dresses for all of us girls. You could order suits for you and Tommy."

"Ten years from now, nobody will know whether we wore new stuff. Let's just wear our best and enjoy our wedding." Jeb shook his head. "As far as I'm concerned, December 20 can't come soon enough."

It was a crisp sunny morning. Nancy, Tommy, and Mary Ann sat on the wagon bench beside Granny, who drove her team to the front of the building. Nancy thanked her Heavenly Father for the little church, which stood as a beacon of all that was true, pure, and lovely in their community. She loved the wreaths of cedar on the double doors of the church.

No one had enough money to buy red ribbons if any had been available. When the mercantile was in business, she had bought fabric there. The store was permanently closed now because Felton Oglethorpe, the owner, remained in the psychiatric ward in the state hospital. His sister and brother-in-law had boarded up the store. Now it was necessary to go to Mize to shop for essentials. For bows, the women constructed ribbons from squares of cloth similar to quilting scraps.

Granny, Nancy, Tommy, and Mary Ann arrived early. A couple of minutes after Granny tethered her horses, Jeb and Evie pulled up in the surrey and parked beside them. Jeb secured his team. The horses, well acquainted with one another, settled in for the wait.

Nancy felt butterflies inside because of excitement and a tinge of uncertainty. She stole a glance at her beloved Jeb. As their eyes met, she couldn't resist telling him, "You look very handsome."

"And you, my dear, look beautiful." He winked.

"Greetings and hugs are in order." Granny's laughter bubbled forth like the rapids of Cohay Creek. "You'd think we hadn't seen one another in weeks, but today is one of the most special in all our lives."

The inside of the church was decked out with mistletoe, bay leaves, and holly intertwined with more bows. The fragrance of Christmas filled the air. The woodburning potbellied stove in the middle of the church made the sanctuary cozy.

"Let's sit near the front." Nancy started the procession.

Quickly the church filled until no places remained. As the congregation overflowed, the deacons brought chairs from the Sunday School rooms. Joy echoed through the pews. Nancy started to correct her family for looking around, but she found herself turning her head to smile at her friends.

The choir assembled in the three elevated pews behind the piano. They sang Christmas carols instead of the usual hymns. Each line of the familiar carols reflected the deep meaning of the holiday. When the congregation joined the choir singing "Joy to the World," Nancy fell in love with Jeb's lyrical baritone voice all over again.

Pastor Barlow preached about love's enduring power. He cleverly blended the message of God's love with the sacredness of the love of a man and his bride. At the end, the pastor requested, "Would the deacons come forward and assist with serving the Lord's Supper?"

After the congregation received communion, Granny led Evie and Tommy to stand in front of the altar while Miss Susannah played softly. Jeb accompanied Nancy, baby Mary Ann in her arms, as they walked to stand before Reverend

Barlow. Before the wedding ceremony began, Nancy passed the sleeping infant to Granny Willietta.

After they spoke their vows, Jeb reached into his shirt pocket for the rings. Nancy's hands came to her mouth. "Oh, how beautiful!"

Smiling with an unrestrained expression of love, Jeb slipped the ring onto her finger and handed her his ring so she could place it on his.

"But how?" She couldn't hold back her tears as she lightly touched the ring he'd placed on her finger.

He whispered, "It's the stone you found."

Pastor Barlow addressed the congregation. "You're all invited to share a Christmas celebration with Mr. and Mrs. McAllister at their new home."

Outside the church, Jeb helped Evie into Granny's wagon. "Tommy, could you go with them and help watch after Evie?"

"Yes, sir."

Jeb assisted Nancy to load in the surrey with Mary Ann in her arms. "We'll have to hurry to get home before the guests start arriving."

Soon flames danced in the fireplaces, and Jeb coaxed the embers in the stove.

Nancy, Jeb, and Granny had prepared enough food for the crowd, but the guests brought more. The women who attended presented Nancy and Jeb with dinner plates, one unique plate from each home stack, as wedding gifts.

Steve Bynum asked Nancy, "Where's the family Bible?"

One more thing brought joy to Nancy's face. "We now have two. Could you record our marriage in both?"

"I'd be delighted." He followed her to a table in the corner of the parlor.

Jeb stood behind Nancy, his hands placed around her waist. "Thanks, Steve, for the ways you have helped us commemorate our marriage. We'll treasure what you are writing here, and the rings will be a symbol of our commitment."

It was a time of happiness and goodwill, all the community full of Christmas cheer. The party lasted until midafternoon.

As the evening approached, Nancy and Granny started out the door to do the farm chores while Jeb stayed with the children. He protested. "I hate it's this way."

Nancy drew her lips into a tight line. "We have to allow your arm time to heal. So far, it's doing pretty good. We can't stop taking care of you now."

After Granny and the children slept, Nancy and Jeb spent precious time together in intimacy. In the middle of the starry night, he held her in his arms. "I'm a simple man, one who means what he says. Today I promised to love you as long as we live, and I will keep my word."

Nancy spoke softly to Jeb. "And I will always love you. Times may be hard, but every day I spend with you will be precious."

Chapter 33

"Jeb, dearest, I dreamed about heaven last night." Nancy pulled her knees up as she took her time moving from the bed.

Jeb pulled her back into the bed for a good morning kiss.

"I dreamed I was holding Amos's hand."

"What?" Jeb sat up.

"We were strolling on the golden streets."

"Really?" He turned toward her and frowned.

"One of my hands was holding Amos's hand, and the other was holding yours."

A smirk flashed across his face. "That's better."

"And your other hand was holding your first wife Mary Ann's."

Jeb pulled Nancy close.

"Love was all around us, but it wasn't like the kind of love…"

He kissed her. "Breakfast can wait."

As they sat at the table, he stirred his coffee a long time. "You want to hear what I dreamed?"

"Sure."

"In my dream me and you sat on the front porch. Two old folks with grandchildren playing all over the yard."

THE END

About the Author

Mary Lou Cheatham grew up near Hot Coffee, Mississippi. She has served as both an educator and a registered nurse. Presently, she resides on the edge of a picturesque canyon in west Texas. She has published inspirational fiction, set in modern and historical times. Her books are listed on her Amazon Author page and at Audible.com.

Acknowledgements

Three or four times a week I take a walk with my daughter Christie Underwood and my son-in-law Brandt Underwood. They faithfully listen to my current ideas about the novel I'm writing and make suggestions. In this way, they support my occupation. In many other ways, they encourage me to enjoy life.

Kathy McKinsey, my editor, knows the story almost as well as I do. How could I complete any project without her help? Kathy has written and published *Gifts of Grace* and *All My Tears*.

Regina Rodgers, the author of *The Gamble on Love*, has been a critique partner throughout the writing of *All Her Dreams of Love*.

Jonni Rich, the author of *The Chartres House Murders*, is my dear mentor. Her mental acuity and knowledge of writing amaze me. She served as a beta reader. Her opinions are priceless.

Sarah Walker Gorrell, who co-authored *Travelers in Painted Wagons* with me, has lived near the banks of Cohay Creek. She understands the story of *All Her Dreams of Love* at a deep level since she has inherited generational knowledge of Mississippi life. She has helped me understand my story as I wrote it.

The American Christian Fiction Writers critique group guided me through every chapter week after week. Their suggestions and critical comments were priceless.

My parents, Myrtle and Robert Gregg, remain the greatest story tellers I've ever known. As early as I can remember, I sat by the fireplace or on the front porch and listened to them. They understood the structure of creating an entertaining tale. They brought life in south Mississippi in the late 1800s and 1900s alive for me.

My great grandmother, whom I never knew, was Nancy Catherine Riley. Some of the events told in *All Her Dreams of Love* resemble what happened in her life. More importantly, my mother taught me the values her grandmother exemplified. In this novel, I have attempted to capture the resilience mixed with a fun-loving spirit of my great grandmother. It's been a blessing to know about her.

Amazon Publishing Plus deserves special recognition for showing me how to take my writing to a new level.

Most of all, I thank my Heavenly Father for providing me the opportunity to sit inside my lovely home and write as much as I please…and for the stamina to continue to write.

Made in United States
Orlando, FL
08 September 2023